POUND OF HORSEFLESH

Clint stepped around the wagons and walked toward the trees. Sure enough, Eclipse came running from the spot where Clint had left him, soon to be followed by a man of average build brandishing a pistol and a noticeable limp.

"I'm gonna kill that damn horse," he screamed while sighting down the barrel at Eclipse's back.

Clint was moving before he even realized what he was doing. Not giving a second thought to who else was out there or what they might think when they saw him, he rushed from the row of wagons and focused his eyes on the man who'd threatened Eclipse.

In one fluid motion, he drew the Colt, pointed and fired . . .

DON'T MISS THESE
ALL-ACTION WESTERN SERIES
FROM THE BERKLEY PUBLISHING GROUP

THE GUNSMITH by J. R. Roberts
Clint Adams was a legend among lawmen, outlaws and ladies. They called him . . . the Gunsmith.

LONGARM by Tabor Evans
The popular long-running series about Deputy U.S. Marshal Long—his life, his loves, his fight for justice.

SLOCUM by Jake Logan
Today's longest-running action Western. John Slocum rides a deadly trail of hot blood and cold steel.

BUSHWHACKERS by B. J. Lanagan
An action-packed series by the creators of Longarm! The rousing adventures of the most brutal gang of cutthroats ever assembled—Quantrill's Raiders.

DIAMONDBACK by Guy Brewer
Dex Yancey is Diamondback, a Southern gentleman turned con man when his brother cheats him out of the family fortune. Ladies love him. Gamblers hate him. But nobody pulls one over on Dex. . . .

WILDGUN by Jack Hanson
The blazing adventures of mountain man Will Barlow—from the creators of Longarm!

TEXAS TRACKER by Tom Calhoun
Meet J. T. Law: the most relentless—and dangerous—manhunter in all Texas. Where sheriffs and posses fail, he's the best man to bring in the most vicious outlaws—for a price.

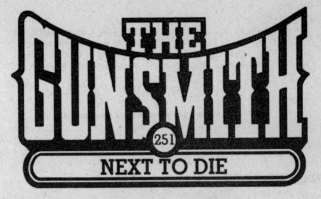

THE GUNSMITH

251

NEXT TO DIE

J. R. ROBERTS

JOVE BOOKS, NEW YORK

NEXT TO DIE

A Jove Book / published by arrangement with
the author

PRINTING HISTORY
Jove edition / November 2002

Visit our website at
www.penguinputnam.com

ISBN: 0-515-13407-4

A JOVE BOOK®
Jove Books are published by The Berkley Publishing Group,
a division of Penguin Putnam Inc.,
375 Hudson Street, New York, New York 10014.
JOVE and the "J" design
are trademarks belonging to Penguin Putnam Inc.

PRINTED IN THE UNITED STATES OF AMERICA

10 9 8 7 6 5 4 3 2 1

ONE

Clint Adams liked the thought of going wherever the wind took him. Just like sailors from the old days, he found the notion appealing that he could travel wherever he liked. Not knowing where he was going next was always part of the charm of his life. And since his life came complete with men taking shots at him on a near regular basis, Clint allowed himself the occasional luxury.

The life of a wanderer offered him freedom, which was something more satisfying than a good meal or soft bed. All he needed to keep it up was a strong horse and the will to keep moving. Eclipse was such a horse and the Darley Arabian stallion seemed to prefer moving down the trail just as much as the man who rode on his back.

Indeed, following the wind was a mighty fine prospect. But every once in a while, even the finest of prospects lost their appeal. No matter how good it sounded most of the time, every idea had its bad moments. Following the wind was a pretty good idea as long as the wind decided to work with you rather than against you. On this particular day, Clint felt as though the wind was definitely against him.

It was the dead of winter on one of those days that

made it more than obvious where that particular term had come from. The ground was covered in snow, which had melted just enough to soak all the way down where it could freeze into something harder than mortar, turning the banks into solid, slanted walls. The trees which poked up from the snow looked like they'd been dead for years, even though they would somehow manage not only to thaw in spring, but blossom as well.

Spring was a long way off, however. In fact, from Clint's point of view, the next season might as well have been the next century. His mind knew that warmth would melt all this snow in a few months, but his body didn't want to hear it. All he knew was that, despite the layers formed by his coat, scarf, hat, gloves, boots, shirt and jeans, his skin felt damn close to shattering like the frozen crust of a lake and falling off of bones which had bits of ice instead of marrow.

The wind no longer acted as a guide. Instead, it hissed in his ears like a coyote that gnawed on every one of his extremities. Over the last couple of minutes, he'd passed the time by counting off on his fingers and toes as, one by one, they tingled and went numb. His muscles felt as though they were getting thicker beneath his skin. Every movement was accompanied by the pricking of invisible needles and it was all he could do to keep himself from shaking so hard that he fell from Eclipse's saddle.

He'd crossed the border into Pennsylvania nearly two days ago. Since he hadn't been this far north or east for some time, Clint thought it would be interesting to head in that direction and check in on some old friends. Along the way he'd be able to visit some places that he hadn't seen for years. It was another one of those ideas that had seemed like a good one at the time.

Of course, Clint knew that the winters could get rough in this part of the country, but he had spent so much time in the southern states lately that he had come to miss the feel of cold air. Having had his fill of sandy ground and hot days, Clint was ready for some good old-fashioned cold.

The autumn had been comforting and the chill in the air had felt nice, so Clint had kept right on moving. Just going where the wind took him and allowing himself to enjoy the ride.

All too quickly, though, the wind had turned into a screeching set of claws, which tore through his gear and turned his blood to ice water. And the worst part of it all was something that Clint had been trying not to think about for the last twelve hours or so.

After riding for so many years over nearly every inch of the country, Clint had a good idea of how to get nearly anywhere he wanted to go. Even now, while he'd been wandering without too much of an agenda, he'd had his sights set on the next town he knew to be in his path.

But that was before the snow had started to fall.

The trail that Clint had been using was one of the major ones in the area and he knew it well. In fact, the trail was fairly well-known by anyone who knew anything at all about the area. He knew exactly where it headed and even had a good idea about where to expect the next town along the way.

But that had been before the snow started to fall.

As of a couple days ago, the trail had become covered with white powder which had been blown across the land in a steady torrent. After that came the drifts, soon followed by the ice, which had thrown everything into a deep freeze.

Now, the trail was lost beneath the thick layer of solid winter, and it would take a team of miners with iron picks and the skin of a grizzly bear to brave the cold and uncover the path once again. And since nobody fitting that description had taken it upon themselves to dig through the snow and make traveling easier, Clint had been relying on his knowledge of the country as well as on his sense of direction.

Although he hated to doubt either of those things, Clint had been getting a creeping feeling in the back of his mind. That feeling perched on his shoulders and caused his guts to twist whenever he saw an unfamiliar ridge or a strange set of hills.

Finally, after delaying it for far too long, Clint admitted the truth to himself: He was lost. And the biting cold, which penetrated him all the way to the core of his body, was an all-too-painful reminder of that fact.

Now that Clint had finally admitted this to himself he pulled back on Eclipse's reins and brought the stallion to a halt. He knew that it would be dangerous to allow the horse to keep still for too long in the cold, but there was something Clint had to do before he could go forward another inch.

He pulled down the part of the scarf that had been wrapped around the bottom part of his face and allowed the wind to tear into his exposed flesh. Lifting his chin and taking a deep breath, he gathered up all of his emotion and set it free.

"God damnit!"

Once that was done, he felt better. No warmer or any less lost, but a hell of a lot better.

TWO

"Did you hear that?"

Sitting on the back of a wagon with his feet hanging down over the edge, Gordon Merrick rubbed his hands together and stared down at the little campfire which was fighting for its life in the icy wind. "Hear what?" he asked.

Standing at just under six feet tall, his muscular frame wrapped in thick furs and heavy cotton, Cam Winslow gritted his teeth and let out an annoyed breath. The exhale emerged as steam from between his lips, sounding like a train's engine as heard from a mile away. "I swear I heard something just now. Could've been someone trying to flank us from the south . . . or even sneak up on us from the southwest."

Gordon shook his head and blew into his cupped hands. "Or it could've also been the same damn ghosts you've been hearing since we left town. Every time I turn around, you're tellin' me or some of the other boys that we got someone followin' us. It ain't doin' a whole lot of good, you know."

"You wouldn't say that if it was true."

"No, I wouldn't. But if it was true, then I might've heard something by now myself, wouldn't I?"

Cam didn't seem to notice the cold air whipping through the camp or even the icicles which had already started to form inside his thick, bristly beard. But he did seem to be mighty annoyed by the turn the conversation had taken. In fact, that weighed heavier on him than the underlying groan which seemed to filter throughout the entire camp.

"Maybe I'll just keep to myself, then," Cam said in a sulking grumble.

Looking up, Gordon pulled the corners of his mouth up into a wide, fake smile. "You know something?" he asked as his chapped lips cracked with several bloody cuts. "I would like that just fine. In fact, I'd say that's the best damn idea you've had in your whole life."

In an odd sort of way, that seemed to settle Cam's nerves more than anything else. He let out another breath and trudged over to the wagon where Gordon was sitting. When he lifted himself onto the back of the wagon, the entire cart squeaked in protest while lowering another couple of inches toward the ground.

Both men sat in their spots and looked down at the fire. Since the flames were just about to die, neither of them bothered to hunker down closer to them. Instead, they gazed down at the remnants of the fire and took what little enjoyment they could from just the sight of it. At least they could be reminded about what it was like to be warmer.

The seconds moved just as slowly as everything else in the cold. After less than a minute had managed to creep by, Cam reached into the lining of his innermost coat and removed a small flask made from dented tin. After pulling off the cap, he was careful not to touch the metal to his lips as he tilted the flask back and poured some of its contents down his throat. The whiskey felt cold at first, but quickly made a turn for the better once the alcohol had a chance to work its magic upon his innards.

"Ahhh." Cam grunted as the whiskey traced a warm, winding path down his throat. "That's the stuff." Without looking over, he held the flask out and offered it to the man next to him.

Gordon accepted it and took a hearty swallow. Waiting for the liquor to make itself known inside of him, Gordon bared his teeth in a tight grimace, which softened into a grin once he finally felt what he'd been waiting for. "Hot damn, where the hell did you get that?"

"I've been saving that since we left Boston. Figured we could partake once this run was over, but figured it could do us some good now."

"If I'd have known you were holding that stuff back, I might have put a bullet in your hide."

"And what about now?"

"Now, I guess I'll have to settle for another sip." After lifting the flask in a silent toast to its owner, Gordon drank some more of the whiskey and then handed it back. "So what did you hear this time?" he asked again, this time with a little less aggravation in his voice.

"Could've been the wind, I guess. But I can tell you one thing . . . the other boys are getting spooked."

Besides the two men sitting on the back of the wagon, there were nine other figures huddled in several small groups near two other wagons. None of the carts were as big as a stagecoach, but all of them were loaded down with so many supplies that they had little room to bounce when they hit a bump in the road. Most of the wagons' contents were in tightly sealed wooden boxes, but there were a few sacks of food and camping gear kept within easy reach toward the rear. The wagon where Gordon and Cam were talking was easily the biggest and was also the only one that was covered with a thick tarp.

Gordon glanced at the other men while rubbing his hands briskly together. The camp had the thick, perfect silence that could only happen in the cold. It was almost as though the sounds that were normally present had been frozen along with everything else in creation, leaving nothing but the lonely whisper of the wind and the crunching of snow beneath the occasional boot.

"Can't say as I blame the boys for bein' spooked," Gordon said. "They definitely got somethin' to worry about."

Cam nodded. "That, they do. If not, we wouldn't have any business bein' this far away from a warm fire and some hot soup."

Allowing those words to filter through his cold ears, Gordon looked back down at the little fire he'd managed to build just as the last spark gave in to the passing wind. When that final flicker of light died away, there was nothing left but a wisp of black smoke. And soon, even that was taken by the chill.

"Tell me somethin', Cam."

"Name it."

"How long do you think it will be before we catch up to the reason that we're out here?"

The bigger man shrugged, but hardly any movement at all could be seen from beneath the layers of furs he was wearing. "Could be days. Could be hours. All I know for sure is that it'll be soon."

"I've got a bad feelin' that it's gonna be sooner than we think."

THREE

After spending so much time on Eclipse's back, Clint could feel the movement of the stallion's muscles changing as the temperature dropped down even further. Although the Darley Arabian did his level best to keep making his way through the thick, fallen snow, his steps were getting slower and his sides were starting to heave a bit more with the increasing effort.

Clint was aware of just how Eclipse was feeling. He felt bad for driving the horse in such miserable conditions, but for the time being he simply didn't have any other choice. "You're doing great, boy," he said while reaching out to vigorously rub the stallion's neck. "If I had my say, I'd put a roof over both of our heads, but that's just not the case right now. I thought for sure there was a town close by, but . . ."

Leaving his sentence unfinished, Clint knew what he was going to say, but didn't even want to hear the words spoken out loud. Rather than bring his attention back to his uncomfortable circumstances, he simply allowed the thought to fade away. At least that way, he could keep some part of him away from the knot, which continued to grow in the pit of his stomach.

As though he was drawing strength from the feel of Clint's hand and the sound of his voice, Eclipse started to quicken his pace through the frozen drifts. The stallion's muscles were aching, but the effort still felt better than letting his bones freeze in place. Before he could get going too fast, however, Eclipse felt the gentle tug of the reins which caused him to reflexively bring his pace down a notch.

"Easy boy," Clint said. "You'd better save your strength. Something tells me you're going to need every bit of it before the day's out."

It wasn't long before Clint dropped down from the saddle so he could walk in front of Eclipse, leading the stallion while he gave his own muscles a bit of a stretch. At first, Clint felt his feet starting to ache. Then, jagged pain sliced through them and ran all the way up his legs. The sensation felt deceivingly warm, but he knew better than to trust it. Clint could tell his body was simply reacting to the conflicting messages that were coming in from his brain as well as the world around him.

The cold wind and icy snow told him to rest. Just have a seat and close your eyes. Maybe even sleep. It would feel so good just to stop moving and stop fighting so hard against the cold.

His brain, on the other hand, was telling him something completely different: Keep moving. No matter how much it hurt to strain muscles that were growing stiff with the cold or pull on tendons that felt ready to snap like frozen leather, he knew he had to keep moving.

He'd heard that dying in the cold was a peaceful way to go. It was just like falling asleep, some folks said. Not much in the way of pain. You would just get real tired and then just sort of drift away. By the time death actually came, you would be halfway delirious anyway. Crossing over that way was just like a dream.

At least that was what he'd heard.

As far as stories regarding death and dying, Clint couldn't allow himself to put much stock in them. The way he saw it, the only ones who could say whether or not those stories were true were in no condition to do much talking. Besides, in Clint's mind, pain or fear didn't really factor into the matter.

Dead was dead.

That was the important thing. And since Clint didn't want to be dead, he knew that he had to ignore the impulses creeping in from the cold and focus on the ones that came from inside his mind. And since his mind was only saying one thing to him, it wasn't too hard for Clint to decide on what he should do.

"Keep moving," he said to himself as well as to the horse behind him. "But save your strength. We're going to need it."

Although he'd said those words before, Clint didn't waste the energy needed to come up with something else. Talking was just a way to keep his jaw from freezing shut and the phrase gave him something else to focus on besides the swirling white, which seemed to close in on him tighter and tighter with each second that passed. The fog that curled up from his mouth hung in front of Clint like a misty veil that was broken with every step he took.

"Keep moving," he whispered.

Although he didn't know the name of the place, Clint was certain that there was a town not too far away. Since he knew he couldn't have been lost for very long, he knew that there had to be a place to get some shelter fairly soon. Even if it meant trekking for an entire day in the snow, it would be worth it if the day could end with him warming his feet in front of a roaring fireplace.

On the other hand, he also knew that going off course even a few degrees could possibly make the difference between being in front of that fire and spending the night in the middle of the frozen wilderness. That thought sat like a piece of rotten meat in his gullet. It festered there until Clint was forced to stop, pull his scarf down from over his face once again and fill his lungs with cold, unfiltered air.

Eclipse ignored the fact that Clint had stopped and bumped into his back with the end of his nose. Shaking the snow that had collected on top of his head, the stallion let out a snuff of air and nudged Clint again.

"I know," Clint said while reaching back to rub the side of Eclipse's head. "We've got to keep moving."

If he was going to say anything else at that moment, Clint quickly forgot. Suddenly, his eyes widened and he let Eclipse's reins slip from his hand. All this time, he'd been keeping his attention fixed upon the sun's placement in the sky as well as the various landmarks which were positioned around him. So far, his only concern was getting himself back where he wanted to be . . . and it had almost made him overlook the most obvious of things.

Smoke.

Not clouds or even the steam of his own breath, the haze rose up in the air and spread out to form a slender cone shape in the sky. It came from a couple of different sources and was easy enough to overlook since his vision had been washed out after spending the day with the sunlight bouncing off the blindingly white landscape. But now that he saw it, Clint looked at the traces of rising smoke and figured the source had to be less than a mile or so away.

Where there was smoke, there was fire.

That thought alone was enough to energize his muscles and chase away any notion he'd had about allowing himself to rest. Even though it would have been nice to give himself and Eclipse a break, Clint decided that it would be more than worth it if he could get to those fires and possibly even get something hot inside his belly.

It was hard to say whether those fires were coming from

the town he'd been hoping to find, but at this point it was more important for Clint to get to any town that he could. Once he was there, it would be a simple matter of asking the right person to figure out exactly where he was and just how far he'd wandered astray.

Clint pulled the scarf back over his face and hooked it over his nose. Picking up Eclipse's reins from where he'd dropped them, he set his eyes on those columns of smoke and headed in that direction. The land became rougher in that new direction and the ground sloped a bit more, which made the travel a little harder. But Clint suddenly felt charged enough to take these obstacles in stride.

After all . . . once he got to those fires, he knew his day could only get better.

FOUR

The instant Cam's boots touched the snow again, he was back into the frame of mind that set him apart from nearly every other man in the group. Not even Gordon was as experienced with the cold and snow as the big man who wore enough furs on his back to blend in with a pack of wolves.

Cam's steps were high and strong, and he took them without once slipping upon the frozen turf. His arms slid easily beneath his wrappings where one hand came to rest upon the handle of his knife and the other settled upon the butt of his .38 caliber revolver. He was the only man who didn't look away when the wind came whipping in his direction. In fact, he seemed to relish the feel of it upon his face.

Gordon didn't mind one bit that his partner was showing him up in this damnable weather. After all, this was why Cam was with them in the first place. It wasn't important for Gordon to impress the others; he'd already done that several times over throughout the years. All that mattered anymore was that they follow him. And if they were all still accounted for in the middle of this frozen

14

bitch of a storm, he figured they'd more than proven their loyalty.

After scooting to the edge of the wagon, Gordon pushed off and dropped down onto the ground. A long, dark-gray coat swung down to brush against the backs of his ankles, setting off a miniature downfall as all the snow that had collected upon his shoulders fluttered upon the ground. He wasn't the biggest man in the group by a long shot. He wasn't even the strongest. But that didn't matter one bit in the eyes of his men.

Gordon's lean, sinewy frame was completely hidden beneath the layers of clothing he wore. Old black boots clung to his feet like dirt to a wagon wheel just as the holster around his waist hugged his hips after having rested in the same spot for over fifteen years. The Smith and Wesson .44 had seen him through much harder times than these and had the notches on its handle to prove it.

Thick dark-brown hair hung down to his shoulders, sprouting from beneath a well-worn Stetson. Gordon's left eye was covered by a black patch, which had frozen to the skin of his face a couple days earlier. Slipping his hands into a pair of riding gloves, Gordon flexed his fingers repeatedly to keep his joints from freezing up within the chilled material. Before too long, the blood was flowing and his hands inside the gloves were warming up just as he'd started walking around the perimeter of the camp in the opposite direction Cam had taken.

The other nine members of the group had already seen Gordon and Cam making their preparations to leave and didn't need to be told that it was their time to follow suit. By the time either of the first two had come to them, the remaining men had kicked snow onto their campfires and were stowing away whatever gear they'd taken from the wagons.

As they walked, Gordon and Cam nodded to the men and returned whatever greetings were tossed their way.

But more than any of that, they were looking toward the horizon surrounding the spot they'd chosen to rest. There wasn't much in the way of trees and the terrain was fairly flat for at least half a mile in every direction. Even though they weren't going to spend more than a few hours in that spot, such things had had to be carefully considered before the small caravan had been allowed to stop.

Gordon had seen too many things happen when he'd let his guard down for even so much as a second. Until this job was over, there would be no rest. Not for him and not for any of his men. Every one of them knew it had to be that way, just like every one of them knew that they might be the next one to leave the party.

Another ten or fifteen paces, and Gordon would have completed his circle around the campsite. He stopped just short of his goal, however, when he spotted something in the distance. "Cam," he said in a carefully measured voice. "Get over here."

The bigger man made his way over to Gordon's side in a matter of seconds. Despite the fact that he easily outweighed Gordon by no less than thirty pounds, Cam hardly made a sound until he opened his mouth to speak. "What is it?"

"There," Gordon said, lifting his hand to point toward the southwest. "Right in between them two trees. Do you see it?"

Cam squinted in the direction the other man was pointing. As he waited, his body became still as a statue. His eyes glistened with a light that came from both inside and out. Finally, after a few seconds had ticked away, he let out the breath he'd been holding and nodded. "Yeah. I see it all right. That's about where I heard that noise comin' from earlier. You still think I should keep my foolish notions to myself?"

"Actually, yes," Gordon replied. "Keep yer foolish notions to yerself. All I want to hear are the good ones. And

warning me about that ghost you heard that's been followin' us just happened to turn out to be one of the good
ones."

Allowing silence to once again wash over him, Gordon
focused his eyes on the same spot and waited again. And
just like before, when the clouds passed over the sun in
just the right way, he saw the same thing that had caught
his attention only moments ago.

There was the field of white, which hurt his eyes the
more he looked at it, broken only slightly by the trees
scattered across the landscape. In the middle of that, ap-
pearing for less than a fraction of a second, there was the
flicker of light, which caused the bottom to drop out of
both Cam and Gordon's stomachs.

"How about you tellin' me exactly what it was you
heard a while back," Gordon said.

"Sounded like a twig snapping. After that, I heard a
metal clicking."

"Kind of like someone working a rifle lever?"

"Yep," Cam replied with a curt nod. "Something like
that."

Without having to say another word, both men dropped
to the ground and pressed themselves flat against the
snow. They didn't even feel the bite of the frozen water
when it came into contact with their skin. What they could
feel was the chill that went down their spines as a gunshot
cracked from the distance and a bullet hissed through the
air over their heads.

"All right, boys," Gordon shouted. "Time to earn your
keep!"

FIVE

Clint was just approaching a stand of trees when he heard the shot echo through the still, cold air. Since he'd first picked up the faint traces of voices coming from the distance, Clint had been straining his ears to catch whatever else he could that might lead him to his destination a little quicker. Because of that, the gunshot sounded like an explosion had gone off right next to his head, which caused him to recoil slightly as his hand went reflexively for the Colt at his side.

But before he cleared leather, Clint shook out the initial reaction and steeled himself for whatever might be coming next. Although he wasn't quite sure what to expect, he could tell that the shot had not been aimed at him. At least that meant that he had the opportunity to play one of the best cards there was in a fight: surprise.

With the gunshot still rolling through the air and in the back of his mind, Clint loosely wrapped Eclipse's reins around a tree branch. It wouldn't be enough to keep the stallion in place if he truly wanted to run, but it was enough to let Eclipse know that Clint wanted him to stay put. Following Clint's lead without question, Eclipse waited patiently behind while Clint continued to move forward.

With his hand still resting on the Colt's handle, Clint kept his head down and took careful steps between the bare trees. Rather than set his feet straight down, he pointed his toe down and slid it into the snow so that he didn't announce his presence with loud, crunching steps. It wasn't the steadiest way to move, but it was quietest. And for the moment, being quiet was all Clint needed.

The trees might not have been dense enough to provide complete cover, but there were enough of them to keep him from seeing clearly through to what was beyond them. As he moved from one trunk to another, Clint kept his eyes searching up and down, shifting between the space in front of him as well as the ground directly ahead.

It didn't take long for him to spot something that caught his interest. Apparently, he wasn't the only one who'd decided to use this place for cover.

The set of tracks he found were obviously fresh since they still retained the shape of a boot despite the snow which drifted down in a steady dusting from the clouds. Also, they'd been pressed in at an angle, meaning that whoever had made them was walking in roughly the same manner as Clint.

Putting himself on the lookout for any sign of movement, Clint lifted his nose slightly and took a deep breath. He tested the air as best he could and was immediately glad he did. Although his sense of smell was nowhere near his strongest asset, even he was able to pick out the acrid odor of freshly burnt gunpowder.

He had yet to hear another shot, so that meant that whoever had fired off that last round had done so from this spot.

This time, when another gunshot cracked through the air, Clint wasn't taken by surprise. Since he'd been expecting more shots, this one didn't even startle him. What

did surprise him was that the shot didn't sound as though
it had been taken anywhere near this area. Even though
the two sounded alike, this shot came from at least twenty
yards to Clint's left.

Moving quicker now, Clint remained alert while still
trying to find traces of the shooter who seemed to be on
the move. Sure enough, before he got to the edge of the
tree line, Clint saw more footsteps. These were different,
however, since they were spaced farther apart and only
the front half of the boot had made an impression.

The shooter had started running. No surprise there.

Clint made it to the edge of the trees and stopped before
breaking from cover. Instinctively, he pressed his back to
a thick trunk and dropped into a squatting position. Once
there, he glanced around the tree and into a large clearing
where a few wagons and several men were gathered. In
the blink of an eye, he knew that the shooter had been
aiming toward those men. And in the next blink, he knew
that those men were just about to start shooting back.

Jerking his head back behind the tree, Clint cursed silently under his breath half a second before the first volley
of gunshots barked out from the group of men in the clearing. This time, there was no mistaking what their target
was as round after round of hot lead whipped between
the trees and chewed into the trunks. Unsure as to who
these men were, Clint decided to hold off before returning
fire. If the bullets kept coming until they dug through the
tree, he might not be able to wait for very long.

Clint looked over toward the rear of the clearing and
took some comfort from the fact that he couldn't see much
of Eclipse through the staggered trunks. At least the Darley Arabian was in slightly less danger than his sole rider.

Suddenly, the section of the tree right above Clint's
head popped as though the bark itself had been rigged to
explode. Splinters flew off in every direction, some of
which bounced off the rim of Clint's hat. Another pop

came after the first and when Clint looked up, he saw that
the shooters in the clearing were starting to take better
aim with rifles that were powerful enough to punch
through the tree.

Clint took a deep breath and drew his Colt. As much
as he didn't like it, he knew he had to either start returning
fire, make a run for it through the blizzard of lead, or sit
where he was and wait for the rounds to get lower until
one of them finally found its mark.

Those were no choices at all. Clint at least took some
comfort from the fact that he was a good enough shot to
keep from killing any of the men intentionally. Of course,
there were always things that could go wrong once the
lead started to fly.

Just as Clint was about to roll away from the tree, he
heard a familiar gunshot coming from someplace other
than the clearing. It was a rifle like the one that had fired
first, only this time it was being fired from even farther
away. The moment it took its shot, the rifle went silent.

Best of all, the other guns went dead as well. And when
they started up again, they were firing to Clint's left rather
than aiming for his skull. Knowing he wasn't going to get
much of a better chance than this, Clint got to his feet,
kept his head low, and broke from cover.

SIX

"Jesus, that one's getting fast," Cam grunted as he ducked behind one of the wagons and thumbed back the hammer of his .38. "I thought we had him pinned down, but he still managed to find another spot."

Gordon was lying on top of one of the carts and was sighting down the barrel of his Winchester rifle. His head bounced back slightly as the gun bucked against his shoulder when he took his shot. Levering another round into the chamber, he glared through the sights once again and shook his head. "Ain't no man can move that fast. I got a look at 'im a second ago over in those trees, but that last shot came from another position."

"So what the hell does that mean?"

"It means that he ain't alone no more. There's at least two of them out there." Gordon paused to squeeze off another shot. His arm worked the lever and was bracing to fire again almost instantaneously. "Maybe more."

Cam shook his head and said, "Jesus Christ. This could be pretty damn bad."

Gordon's only reply was a quick nod. Then he turned to look over his shoulder and bark out commands to the men who were positioned all around him. "Sanchez and

Rico . . . you two keep firin' at them trees. Connoway . . .
take a few others and try to flank whoever took that last
shot. The rest of ya . . . come with me."

"What are you doing?" Cam asked.

But Gordon was already hopping down from the cart.
He barely seemed to notice the other shots that were coming in from the surrounding area. Instead, he waited for
the men to come to him and handed out his orders as
though he was in the middle of a war.

Cam took a pair of men for himself and formed a second team that would cover Gordon's play. Since the other
man seemed bent on making a charge toward the shooters,
the least he could do was try to make sure they came back
alive.

In less than a minute, the men were organized and
ready to go. Gordon was leading his team toward the most
recent source of gunfire and Cam had decided to spread
his group out so they could either move toward the trees
or act as backup for Gordon. Without taking much time
to have any second thoughts, all five men readied their
weapons and ran out from behind the wagons.

As soon as they'd gone, Connoway motioned for his
group to start moving and they headed in a wide arc,
which would hopefully take them behind one of the shooters while Cam and Gordon drew most of the fire. All of
the men in the third group stuck close to the wagons until
they saw that the first two were well into the open. Then,
Connoway quickened his pace and prayed that he wasn't
rushing head-first into a deathtrap.

Gordon didn't concern himself with the shots that came
in. They were too few and far between for him to worry
about them too much. What concerned him more was the
fact that the shots *weren't* coming in at the moment. From
his past experience, that only meant one thing: that the
shooter was taking his time to get a good, careful aim.

"Watch yerselves," he said to his men as they rushed forward. "The moment you see anything, be sure to—"

But the rest of his warning was swallowed up by a popping explosion, came from a small group of low rocks directly ahead of them. There was a puff of smoke and the hiss of a bullet cutting across the distance that separated the shooter from Gordon and his men.

The round flew like an angry hornet toward its target, bit into warm flesh and drilled all the way through until it came out the other side.

The man standing to Gordon's right grunted in pain and dropped to his knees. He reached up with his free hand to grab at a spot on his neck that had suddenly erupted into blinding pain. When he touched the spot, he felt more pain, as well as something hot and warm. Pulling his hand back, the man saw that his glove was covered in blood which had already soaked through the material and was beginning to coat his hand. After that, shock descended on him and his world started to spin.

"Aw hell," Gordon grunted as he looked back toward the fallen man. One of the others had stopped to go to the wounded man's side, but Gordon stopped him with a stern warning. "No! We'll come back for him. Come on!"

The second figure paused for a second, which was just long enough for him to see the gaping bullet hole in his companion's neck. When the wounded man fell forward, it was plain to see that the bullet had passed completely through his neck to leave a hole twice the size of the first just below the base of the man's skull. Blood pumped out of the wound like water from a tipped bucket and his face had turned nearly as white as the snow.

Having only fallen a couple steps behind Gordon and the rest, the other man left the body where it lay and continued his charge. The fire of vengeance burned in his eyes as a battle cry rose up from the back of his throat.

Gordon knew his man was dead. He only had to see

that he'd been hit to figure out that much. It wasn't because of any keen sight or medical knowledge. It was
simply experience that told him to forget about anyone
that fell during one of these charges. After all, why should
this one be any different from the others that had been
hit? None of them had pulled through.

The sniper was too good to leave any of them alive.

Gordon kept moving, but he would never forget about
the man he'd lost. He wouldn't forget about any of them.
He would do the only thing he could do, which was to
remember their names and make sure they hadn't died for
nothing. Once Gordon found that sniper, he would put
him down for good. And before the shooter died, Gordon
would repeat the names of every one of the men who had
been killed so that that murdering son of a bitch would
take those words to hell right along with the rest of him.

Ticking off the time in his head, Gordon pushed himself to run even faster, hoping to cover more ground while
the sniper reloaded and took aim on his next target. Prior
experience also told him that there was precious little time
to waste. In fact, he was expecting to feel the bite of lead
in his own flesh at any moment.

The rocks they were heading toward seemed to get farther away with every step they took. If Gordon wasn't so
familiar with the tricks that stress could play on a man's
senses under fire, he might have sworn that he was trying
to run across a field of ice where every move he made
only yielded half the results that they should.

But he kept moving because that was the only thing he
could do. He'd already committed not only himself, but
the rest of his men to this attack. Foolish or not, they
would all see it through.

Cam pumped his legs as fast as he dared in the thick
layers of snow. Using his momentum to keep his balance
as well as push him forward, he felt like he was constantly

about to topple onto his face and was only caught in the nick of time by the foot that he planted on the ground ahead of him.

He knew he'd seen something moving in those trees. Even after the last shot went off, he swore he saw something moving in this area. It was just a sliver of motion, but it was enough for him to focus on as he led his men toward the trees.

Whatever it was that had moved, Cam swore to himself that it wouldn't be moving for very much longer.

SEVEN

Clint's heart thumped within his chest like a sledgehammer. Every breath he took burned inside his lungs even though the air he was breathing caused his exhales to form steam in front of his face. No longer worrying about stealth, he opted for speed and speed alone as he dashed through the trees and worked his way around to the back of the clearing that he'd spotted.

He knew that he'd been seen. The shots fired in his direction told that tale well enough. He also knew that the shooters were coming for him. All he needed was a set of ears to catch the shouting voices and the beat of footsteps, which pounded against the ground and kicked up a path through freshly fallen snow.

But what Clint wasn't sure about was whether or not he'd been seen making his way through the stand of trees. Although he'd been moving as quickly as possible, he'd also been running from behind one tree trunk to another, attempting to keep as hidden as possible while moving as fast as his legs could carry him.

There had been more shots fired, but he wasn't listening carefully enough to determine if that first rifle was still among them. Instead, Clint's main concern was whether or not he was still a target. And as far as he could tell, the shots were still coming from behind him and no more bullets were whipping through the air in his immediate vicinity.

Rather than think about it any further, Clint simply focused on the ground ahead and kept moving. As those two words kept going through his mind, he couldn't help but notice the irony of hearing the mental command yet again.

Keep moving.

If it wasn't one thing, it was another. If it wasn't being lost in the cold, it was being shot at by unknown gunmen. If Clint ever got a chance to sit still for an hour or two, he swore that he would thank whatever stars that were responsible for his change of pace.

Clint's stomach tensed as he broke free of the tree line and into the open space of the snowy field. There wasn't much more than twenty or thirty yards to cover between the trees and the clearing, but it seemed to be a hell of a lot more than that when the possibility of being shot was looming so low over Clint's head.

Luckily, the area wasn't completely open. There were still rocks and bushes scattered about. All were covered in snow and all provided some small degree of cover for Clint as he made his way toward the clearing and the wagons that were still parked there. Clint ducked down when the opportunity presented itself for him to move behind something that would hide him from any eyes that might be pointed in his direction.

The Colt was back in its holster, freeing up both hands in the very likely event that he hit a patch of ground slippery enough to sweep his legs out from under him. Although Clint would have felt much more comfortable with the gun in his hand, he knew that very thing might also get him shot on sight if he was spotted.

Running his hand along the back of a stout boulder as

he moved around it, Clint took in a deep breath and braced himself for the last dash that would carry him into the clearing. Once he was there, he would have to act fast. Whether it would be talking or shooting, he knew he wouldn't have much time at all to make his move.

Clint knew he would find out the hard way which it would be in a matter of seconds, as he hurried around the farthest wagon and slowed to a quick walk. There was a man crouched behind one of the other wagons whose attention was focused in the opposite direction. Clint was trying to come up with a way to get his attention without startling him too badly when suddenly the matter was taken out of his hands.

Snap

The sound of a revolver's hammer being cocked was unmistakable. And so was the press of a barrel against the small of Clint's back.

"Don't move," came a voice from behind Clint that was tense, yet steady. "Raise them hands, and if you make one move toward that gun, I'll drill a hole through your heart."

Clint was sure to move as nonthreateningly as possible. First, he lifted his arms out to either side with his hands open wide, and then he placed both hands on top of his head. He could feel the other man taking hold of the modified Colt and waited for the moment when the pistol started lifting up out of its holster.

In a motion that was almost too fast to see, Clint spun himself around in a tight circle while bringing one hand in a downward chop. He managed to twist away from the gun just as it went off, his forearm making contact with the other man's wrist.

The impact was quick and very painful, sending jolts of agony through the other man's arm all the way up to his shoulder. He had no choice but to drop the gun as Clint continued his sideways turn.

His back still burning from the blast of the gun he'd

narrowly avoided, Clint followed through with his arm and kept it going all the way down to his holster. Once there, he plucked the Colt from its resting place and jabbed the end of its barrel into the gut of the man standing in front of him.

"I'm not here to hurt anyone," Clint said quickly. "Tell me what's going on."

The other man had dark skin and hair that was black as coal. There was something about him that seemed strange and for a moment, Clint couldn't quite put his finger on what it was. It didn't take him long to figure it out, however. The sight of a Mexican wrapped up like an Eskimo was enough to make any man pause for a second or two.

"Sanchez?" came a voice from the wagons. "Bring that fella over here or shoot him, but be quick about it."

The Mexican stared directly into Clint's eyes and didn't move a muscle. He didn't even flinch when Clint moved the Colt.

"Go on," Clint said as he pulled the gun away and dropped it into his holster. "Bring me over there before your friend gets too agitated."

EIGHT

Cam ran past the first tree and was ready for anything he might find. He kept his gun in front of him and had his finger already tensing on the trigger as he looked around for his target. All he found was empty air and more trees, however. But then he caught a glimpse of that same movement that had brought him over this way in the first place.

Without breaking stride, he motioned for the others to follow him and charged forward. The farther he ran, the more he could see between the trees. Whoever was there wasn't moving much, which meant he probably still thought that he could get a shot off before he was in any danger. That very notion made Cam's blood boil and he raised his guns, preparing to fire.

A split second before it was too late, he let go of the trigger and skidded to a stop. The others who'd been following him bunched up at Cam's back.

"What did you find?" one of the others asked. When he didn't get an answer right away, he took another step forward and moved around a tree to get a look for himself.

"Shit," Cam grumbled as he looked at the target he'd come all this way to shoot. "Shit!"

All of the men were gathered around by this time. Every one of them were staring at the Darley Arabian stallion which stood calmly in the snow just as calm as you please.

Eclipse glanced from one strange face to another, his jaw working on a bit of frozen sod he'd managed to pluck from beneath the snow while waiting for Clint's return.

Cam lifted his pistol and glared down the barrel. "I ought to shoot this damn horse. If he belongs to Jessup, at least he won't be able to carry that back-shooting son of a bitch out of here anytime soon."

Before Cam could pull the trigger, he felt a hand on his elbow. One of the other men stepped in front of him and slowly pushed his gun down until it was pointed away from the horse. "Hold up, Cam. Let's put this horse to work rather than shoot it. We still have to get over to help Gordon and by the time we get there on foot, the fight'll be over."

A tense moment passed before Cam finally released the hammer and holstered the gun. "Fine. Have it your way. Take this animal and ride over to Gordon. I'll meet you there." And before anyone else could say a word, the big man took off running back through the trees. From behind, he resembled a small bear rather than a man, and he moved much faster than either. The furs wrapped around his body flapped in the breeze and he all but disappeared before another man took off after him.

Left to his own devices, the man who had saved Eclipse's life approached the stallion with both hands held in front of him. Even though he knew he had to hurry, he couldn't help but take a moment to look at the Darley Arabian. In all his life, he'd never seen a horse quite as fine as this one. And the closer he got to it, the more he figured on keeping the animal for himself.

"OK, now," he said in the calmest voice he could manage. "Don't be scared . . . ain't about to hurt you."

Eclipse stared back at him with more than a little understanding reflected in his big eyes.

There hadn't been any more shots after the one that had drilled through the last man's throat, but Gordon knew better than to take any comfort from that fact. All something like that told him was that the shooter was either setting up for another kill or had already managed to get away.

In a strange way, Gordon hoped for the former. At least that would mean he still had a chance at getting his hands on the killer after going through so much hard work.

As he thought these things, his legs were still pushing him closer to the small outcropping of rocks. His eyes searched for any trace of movement and his ears were waiting for the slightest sound that didn't belong.

A stray footstep, which didn't come from the men behind him.

The metallic *click* of a bullet being chambered.

A breath that was heavy enough to give away the sniper's position.

Any of these things would have been enough to satisfy Gordon's appetite. And any one of those things would have made losing one more man somewhat less in vain.

Hardly any time at all had actually passed. A few seconds, which added up to less than half a minute was all it took for the small group of men to charge across the short stretch of field, ending one of their lives in the process. Now that they were within spitting distance of the rocks, Gordon held up his hand to let the others behind him know that they should slow down and wait for their target to present itself.

Gordon's gun was steady in his hand, clenched within a fist so tight that his knuckles were turning white beneath his glove. His thumb was hooked over the edge of the hammer, ready to snap it back the instant he had a clear shot.

The rocks came up slightly higher than waist-level, giving whoever was behind them just enough room to keep himself hidden. Crouching down low, the sniper might have been ready to fire around the left side or right. He might have been ready to lash out with a blade. Or, he might have already . . .

Pouncing around the rocks like a bobcat taking down its latest meal, Gordon pulled back the hammer of his Smith and Wesson .44 and pulled his trigger the moment he was able. The gun spat its fiery cargo through the air and into the ground as its explosion rolled outward in every direction.

Gordon's rage was almost enough for him to empty the rest of his shots just so he could vent it. But that wouldn't do him any good since those shots would hit exactly what the first one had: absolutely nothing.

The sniper was gone. And just to make sure Gordon was even more infuriated, the shooter had left a little calling card to make it obvious that he had, indeed, been there.

Gordon reached down and picked up the single spent rifle shell and held it in front of his face. By the way he looked at it, the other men half-expected to see the brass container begin to melt into slag.

NINE

Once Clint had introduced himself properly to the men who'd stayed behind with the wagons, he found that they were perfectly willing to let him stay. Of course, part of those "proper introductions" had included disarming both men with less effort than it would have taken some men to pull on their boots.

Clint could feel the tension in the air the moment he'd gotten close enough to hear both men's voices, which made it that much easier to get the drop on them. They were obviously not unfamiliar with handling a firearm and they even had the look of peacekeepers about them. That made it all the stranger for them to seem so spooked.

Besides the Mexican, there was a young Indian who hardly seemed surprised at all that their camp had been infiltrated. When Clint had announced himself, the Indian made a good effort to try and draw down on the intruder, but Clint was simply too fast for him and soon both of the other men were sitting side-by-side, their guns in Clint's custody.

"Like I said to your friend here," Clint told the Indian. "I'm not here to hurt anyone. And just to prove there's no hard feelings . . ." With a simple gesture, he tossed both men their guns and holstered his own.

Watching the men carefully, Clint was testing them to see just what their intentions were. A lot could be discovered in watching a man react under hard conditions. It was times like that that brought out someone's true nature. The aggressive or impulsive ones would try to fight. The frightened ones would try to run. And the ones who could keep their heads level would try something else. There was no set of rules for what could happen, so Clint decided to stand back and watch to see what *would* happen.

And if all else failed, Clint knew he could outdraw them both.

While each of the men were quick to take up their weapons once they were within reach, neither one of them made a move against Clint right away. Of the two, the Indian seemed more likely to do something, but that stemmed mostly from his youth. The Mexican slipped his finger beneath his trigger guard, looked at Clint, and then took a step forward.

Rather than extend the hand holding the gun, he held out the empty one. "Something tells me you mean what you say. My name's Sanchez."

The Indian's eyes flashed with hostility. "What the hell are you doing? How do you know you can trust him?"

"Because if he wanted to shoot us, he would have done it already," Sanchez replied. Looking back to Clint, he said, "That's Rico. He's a little jumpy, but I'm sure you could understand why. Normally, he would have known that the one we're after likes to kill quickly and from a distance. Besides . . . I think I recognize your face. Do I know you?"

Clint glanced over to Rico. Although the younger man seemed reluctant to accept him just yet, he also didn't seem as close to taking a shot at him as he'd been only seconds ago. All in all, Clint figured that both men had passed the little test he'd given them. But that didn't mean that he was about to let his guard down just yet.

"I might have seen you somewhere," Clint said to Sanchez. "I tend to move around quite a bit. The name's Clint Adams."

Hearing that, both men's eyes widened. Sanchez nodded slightly as a smirk crept over his face. "Ahhh. That's it. I played a few hands of poker with you on a riverboat in Mississippi. That was a year or two back, but I would never forget meeting someone like you. The boat was called the *River Queen*."

Clint smiled. He remembered the boat well. "That was a good night if I recall. Sorry if I don't remember your face. There were a lot of games over those couple of days."

"Well I was one of the men you cleaned out. I'm not surprised you don't remember me. I wasn't at the table for very long," the Mexican said while flashing a group of smoke-stained teeth. "I gave up gambling after that game. You cost me a lot of money, Adams. But a man's got to learn when to give up a bad habit."

Stepping forward, Rico said, "I hate to interrupt your recollections, but there's still some important business to take care of out there. Or did you already forget?"

"Use yer ears, boy," Sanchez growled. "The shooting's stopped. That means the fight's over. Whoever's left will be back shortly."

With that, the Mexican turned away from Clint and walked back toward the wagons. That gesture was his own test, which Clint recognized immediately. Turning your back on an armed stranger was a fighter's show of respect and if it wasn't mishandled, trust was soon to follow.

Clint let the man keep walking before moving up to the wagons himself. Looking down, he saw that Sanchez had his hand on his gun and was ready to draw if Clint had made one wrong move. "So what's all this shooting about?" he asked. "By the sound of it, I thought there was a war going on."

"You're not far from the truth," Sanchez replied. "We got us a little war brewing here. And by the looks of it . . . we got us some more casualties."

Apparently, Rico had seen the same thing as well. "Aww, no," he whispered while squinting toward the outcropping of rocks in the distance.

Following both men's line of sight, Clint took a look for himself and instantly saw what had captured their attention. One man was walking around the rocks, cursing so loudly that some of his words could be heard from where Clint was standing. Between the wagons and those rocks, a couple of others were carrying a body toward the campsite, one man holding the legs and the other holding the arms.

There were some other men rushing toward the rocks from the trees that Clint had been using as a hiding spot who made a straight line directly toward the man that was closest to the rocks. All the gunfire had stopped, except for one shot that rang out from the trees. That sound was followed by another voice swearing at the top of its lungs.

"What the hell?" Rico said as he stepped out from behind the wagon to get a better look.

Sanchez reached out to grab the other man's arm while scolding him in an urgent voice. "Get back here you damn fool! Don't you remember nothing that's been going on around here?"

Rico shook off the Mexican's grip impatiently. "That was Underhill's voice just now. What's got him so riled up that nobody else seems to care about?"

"Who gives a damn. Just get back under cover before you catch a bullet."

Clint observed the way the men acted. Both the ones by the wagons as well as the ones out in the field acted like soldiers on a battlefield. Whatever it was they were after, it had them using combat reflexes along with infantry tactics. By the looks of things, these men that Clint had been talking to were the grunts. The commanders were still on their way back to camp.

Before Clint could ask any more questions, he heard something else that piqued his interest. It wasn't gunshots or even another shouted curse. In fact, it was something that held much more value in Clint's mind than any of those things and it was carried on the frozen wind like an arrow that was meant for his ears alone.

The sound was a drumming thump at first. The beating of hooves upon icy ground. But it wasn't until he caught the distinctive whinny that Clint knew for sure he knew the horse that was making those sounds. It was Eclipse. And somehow, Clint knew that the stallion was awfully worked up about something.

In a flash, Clint stepped around the wagons and walked toward the trees. Sure enough, Eclipse came running from the spot where Clint had left him, soon to be followed by a man of average build brandishing a pistol and a noticeable limp.

"I'm gonna kill that damn horse," he screamed while sighting down the barrel at Eclipse's back.

TEN

Clint was moving before he even realized what he was doing. Not giving a second thought to who else was out there or what they might think when they saw him, he rushed from the row of wagons and focused his eyes on the man who'd threatened Eclipse.

Apparently, the man hadn't even noticed that Clint was there and was still only seconds away from making good on his deadly promise. Clint acted on sheer instinct, although he did have to force himself to hold it back a notch or two.

In one fluid motion, he drew the Colt, pointed and fired. The shot rang out, stopping everyone in the area dead in their tracks.

The man who'd been about to fire on Eclipse stood rooted to his spot, the horse forgotten as Clint's bullet whipped through the air well over his head. Like the others, he was wrapped in warm clothing from head to toe. Dark-blond hair poked out from beneath the edges of his hat, but the stubble growing from his face was a lighter shade and almost invisible against the color of his skin. Also, like all the others, he now swung his gun around to aim squarely at Clint.

The freezing air died down at that exact moment, almost as though the winter wind was waiting to see just how many times Clint was about to get shot. The sound of several hammers being snapped into firing position clattered through the field like some kind of strange snake's rattle.

Moving ever so slowly, Clint lowered his pistol and dropped it into his holster. After that, he raised both hands in the air as the silence became so thick around him it almost seemed to smother him. Clint could feel the tension of all the men, including those who he'd left behind with the wagons. Finally, he broke the quiet with a snap of his fingers and a short, shrill whistle.

Hearing that, Eclipse broke into a gallop and rushed straight over to stand at Clint's side. But Clint still kept his movements short. All he did was reach out to place a hand upon the Darley Arabian's muzzle, rubbing the short, coarse hairs until the stallion's breathing came back down to normal.

One of the other men, a big, bulky specimen who'd been somewhere near the rocks, stalked over to Clint with a pistol gripped in a large paw of a hand. His entire body was wrapped in furs, making him look even more ferocious than he already did. "I don't know who you are, mister, but you'd best not get on that horse."

"Don't worry," Clint said. "I was just trying to keep him from getting shot. That's all."

Cam got a little closer, eyeing Clint as though he was looking at a free meal after going hungry for weeks. Before he could say anything else, he stopped short and stared at the figure who was hurrying up to stand beside Clint.

It was Sanchez. The Mexican approached Cam defensively, but made sure not to put himself between the bigger man and Clint. "This here's Clint Adams. He got here right as all this started and came over to see what was going on."

"Oh?" Cam asked skeptically. "Is that what he told you?"

"Yeah. And I believe him, because I recognized him with my own two eyes. He is who he says he is. And since I know he didn't come all this way in this damn cold on foot, I'd say that that there's his horse."

Studying Clint carefully, Cam watched the way the other man presented himself. But more than that, he watched to see how Eclipse was acting toward him. "I may not be sure about you yet," he said to Clint. "But animals don't know how to lie. Either that is yours or you're one hell of a charmer."

By now, the men carrying the dead body were coming back to camp. They were accompanied by Gordon, who walked straight past them, straight past Cam and didn't stop until he was toe-to-toe with Clint. He stared at the new arrival with fire in his eyes and his hands placed squarely upon his hips. "Who the hell are you?"

"Clint Adams. Do your men make it a habit to hunt down good horses?"

Gordon was too angry to hide the confusion that raced through his mind. His eyes narrowed slightly and his head cocked to one side in a way that reminded Clint of a dog listening to a slide whistle. "Huh? What the blazes are—?"

"It was Underhill," Cam said from behind the other man. "He found that horse over in them trees and wanted to ride it over to cover you by the rocks. I figured it was Jessup's and damn near put it down myself."

Looking between Cam and the blonde named Underhill, Gordon let out an exasperated breath and threw his hands up into the air. "All I want to know is if this here asshole lives or dies," he said, pointing to Clint.

"If he is Clint Adams, then he ain't with Jessup," Cam said.

Gordon let his hands drop. "Fine. He lives. But don't give him any food unless he decides to stay on with us." With that, he brushed past Clint and stomped past the wagons.

Some of the others who were coming in gave Clint looks ranging from curiosity all the way to suspicious. None of them seemed openly hostile, however. Mostly, they seemed tired. Clint knew exactly how they felt.

The only one to stay where they were was Cam. He waited for all the others to move along before stepping up and reaching out to slap a hand on Clint's shoulder. "I've got a feeling that you're exactly who you say you are."

Clint took hold of Eclipse's reins and led the stallion behind him as he followed Cam into the camp. "Really? And what brought about your sudden change of mind?"

Laughing under his breath, Cam made his way toward one of the wagons and said, "Because a man would have to be all kinds of stupid to wander in here at this particular moment and announce himself the way you did to a bunch of armed men. And if you ain't stupid, that only leaves one other possibility."

"What's that?"

"Real unlucky. And there ain't no law against that."

ELEVEN

Jessup had been moving so fast and so silently that he felt like a piece of the wind which had split off from the rest and started thinking on its own. There hadn't been much to use by way of cover except for a scattered bunch of rocks and trees that dotted the frozen landscape like scraggly hairs on an old man's head.

It hadn't been much, but it had been enough to allow Jessup the escape he needed. He was no miracle worker, however. The escape was the product of a well-planned route, which he'd plotted out in the hours before the sun had crested over the horizon. He'd even managed to plant some aids to help him along the way in the form of a horse blanket covered with snow buried at just the right spot.

When he'd been making his way out as Gordon and his men had been coming in, it was a simple matter of waiting for just the right moment and diving under the blanket. Once he'd pressed himself down against the cold ground and pulled in some loose snow to cover his edges, Jessup became just another bump in the landscape. A bump wasn't worth noticing, especially when a man was looking for someone who'd just managed to pick off one of his followers.

Jessup thought about this and chuckled to himself. The front of his body was so cold after being pressed into the snow that he could hardly feel those muscles, but it was well worth the discomfort. He'd accomplished his task and beaten the others so badly that they didn't even bother coming to look for him once they'd lost sight of him.

They knew better than to come after him.

They'd been taught that lesson through the blood of their friends over the course of an entire month.

Jessup loved his chosen profession. Sure, it had its risks, but killing was so much more to him than just a way to earn a living. It was a fine art that allowed him to use every bit of his heart, mind, body and soul. There were plenty of other professional killers out there, but they weren't anything but guns for hire.

Most of those killers were nothing more than pieces of poorly maintained equipment that were good for one thing before falling quickly into disrepair. They were no better than the guns they brandished, which was why they worked so very cheaply.

While Jessup could be rightfully accused of many things, taking human life cheaply was not one of them. When he snuffed a life out, he did so professionally and cleanly. He didn't turn down any job, no matter how distasteful or how big. A life was a life.

Women.

Children.

It didn't matter to Jessup. Either one would get as much of his attention as any man. That was why he could get away with charging fifteen hundred dollars for every job he took. He worked with all the precision of a machine. And, like a machine, he didn't flinch when the time came for him to act.

He hadn't even flinched when he'd taken on his current

job. But this wasn't like any other job he'd taken. In fact, this was more of a duty. More than that . . . it was personal. There was no money involved. His only payment was the satisfaction of sending all of those bastards out there into hell with a fresh hole drilled through their skulls.

Even for him, though, twenty men were a hell of a lot of targets. Especially when they were all experienced gun hands in their own rights. But he didn't see the job as impossible. On the contrary, it was a great challenge. At times it had even been fun.

Today had been the closest Jessup had come to getting hurt. Gordon Merrick had been so close that he could almost hear the other man's breath. He could still feel the thrill of the chase coursing through his blood and he could still hear the curses that had been shouted out when they realized that they'd failed to catch Jessup yet again.

Now that he'd put enough distance between himself and Gordon's camp that he could run for the spot where he'd tied off his horse, Jessup started to feel a bit of disappointment in his gut. It wasn't much. Just the same kind of feeling he got as a kid when all of his anxious waiting had come to an end the day after opening his Christmas present.

He'd made his kill for the day. It was over. All he had to do now was get back to his bed and rest up for the next one. Unlike those wintry days in late December of his youth, he didn't have to wait a whole year before he got to open his next present.

By the time Jessup made it back to his horse and climbed into the saddle, he could no longer hear the excited voices of Gordon Merrick and his men. After securing his rifle in its place strapped to the saddle near his left knee, Jessup pulled the collar of his jacket up to protect himself against the brisk wind and dug his heels into the animal's sides. He snapped the reins for good measure and in a couple of seconds, the horse was plowing through the snow as if its life depended on it.

The town of Allyn's Mill was less than ten miles away and Jessup wanted to be sure and get there as soon as possible. If he wasn't going to do any more shooting, then he figured he had no more business being out in the god-forsaken cold. As he rode, he could feel the chill digging deeper and deeper inside of him until its icy fingers reached all the way down to scrape the inside of his veins.

All the time he'd spent in the elements was starting to catch up to him and though it wasn't a very long ride before he reached civilization, the town seemed to be ten times as far the longer he thought about how good it would be to get there.

Jessup had actually started to like Allyn's Mill. He felt like he belonged there even though nobody who lived in the place knew his name or even who he was. He was looking forward to getting back there once again. Hopefully there would be time to go to confession at the little chapel in town. Confession always made him feel better about himself, especially when the blood was still hot in his veins and fresh on his hands.

Confession was good for the soul.

TWELVE

"Is it just me," Clint asked, "or does everyone here seem just a little too relaxed?"

Cam looked around the camp, which was quiet, yet much busier than it had been just prior to the shootings. Most of the men were stowing what little remained of their gear into the wagons and the rest were harnessing the horses in their place at the head of each cart.

The dead body had also been stored in one of the wagons. It had been wrapped tightly in a bundle of burlap and topped with a simple cross made by two sticks that had been lashed together with twine. Clint took notice of the fact that nobody had even tried to bury the corpse, but didn't feel it was his place to ask anybody why that was.

"Relaxed?" Cam said sarcastically. "Not hardly, Adams."

Clint was reluctant to let go of Eclipse's reins since Underhill was walking on his other side. "That might not be the right word, but I guess it just seems a bit . . ."

"Too much calm after the storm?" Underhill offered.

Clint snapped his fingers. "That's it."

"I know what you mean. But that's only because I just signed on with this group a week ago."

48

Cam laughed at the smaller man. Underhill was by no means a spindly sort, but he didn't come near to the bulk of the bigger man wrapped up in furs. "The German's got a lot to learn, that's for sure. And he should start off with a proper riding lesson."

Not until he'd heard that word come from Cam's mouth did Clint really see the German features in Underhill's face. Now that he took a closer look, it was plain to see the sharp, angled lines in his cheeks, nose and chin. The shape of the eyes was vaguely European and the tint of the hair seemed especially light.

"I know how to ride, Cam," Underhill said in his own defense.

"Yeah, but you don't know some of the finer aspects. Like trying to ride just any strange horse that you find standing around." Turning quickly to Clint, he added, "No offense meant."

Clint smirked at the comment. "None taken. So is that what happened back there? You found Eclipse and tried to climb into the saddle?"

A shadow passed across Underhill's face at the very thought of what had happened. "I did. And the damned beast nearly broke my neck when he threw me. He took off and I guess I lost my temper after that."

Clint didn't even try to suppress the laughter that gurgled up from the back of his throat. Giving Eclipse's neck an extra scratch, he said, "Good boy."

Cam had been watching this conversation with a fair bit of interest. Looking at the way Clint talked to Underhill, he found that his initial distrust of the newcomer was starting to melt away just like the snows around him would pass in the spring. Before too long, he was starting to laugh as well. The sound he made rolled through the quiet frozen air like thunder.

"Just what's so damn funny?" Underhill asked.

As Cam started to reply, he had to stop for a second

because the laughter just kept getting worse. "I'm sorry . . ." he said when he could finally draw a breath. "It's just that you nearly get your ass busted trying to get on that horse and then this fella comes in here and nearly busts it again. He looks like he thinks that horse is smarter than you and I . . ." Cam paused to let another wave of laughter rush through him. ". . . I think I have to agree with him."

Stopping in his tracks, Underhill glared at both men angrily. Finally, he shook his head and turned to walk in the other direction. "Aww, to hell with both of you," he said with a dismissive wave.

There was a thick silence between Clint and the bigger man which lasted for a full two seconds. That was as long as either one could hold out before busting out with full-bodied laughter that drew the attention of everyone else in the camp. Although the rest of the men seemed confused, they turned back to their own business when they saw Cam laughing just as hard as Clint.

"You know something?" Cam said after slapping Clint on the back hard enough to drive most of the air from his lungs. "You're all right. And that horse of yours is a damn fine piece of work."

"I appreciate that. No hard feelings about the way I introduced myself, I hope?"

Cam shrugged and led the way to where one of the wagons was being loaded. "You nearly got yourself shot full of holes for pullin' that stunt. I know that for a fact, because I was the one who almost gave the order to fire. I figure that squares us up."

"Great," Clint said, following the fur-covered man. "Then maybe you can answer the question I've been asking since the moment I set foot in this place."

"I'll see what I can do once I hear what's on your mind."

"All I want to know is what the hell is going on here,

who you people are and why you're all under fire." After thinking for another second, Clint added, "And where are you taking that body?"

Whistling softly as he tossed some gear into the wagon, Cam closed the cart's rear gate and pulled a tarp over the cargo. "That's an awful big mouthful. If you want to hear the answers, you'll have to come along with us. We're about to get a move-on right quick, but you're welcome to tag along."

Clint sighed heavily and tried to mask the frustration he felt as his questions were once again pushed unceremoniously off to one side. "Where are you headed?" he asked.

"There's a town farther down the trail a stretch named Allyn's Mill. We aim to get some more supplies and rest up before heading out again in a day or two. Were you on your way somewhere or just out and about?"

As much frustration as he was feeling at the moment, Clint couldn't help but like the bigger man. Hearing the name of that town gave Clint an idea of where he was. It still bothered him, however, since he actually thought he'd been headed for the town three miles north of Allyn's Mill. "I guess you could say I started out as one and wound up being the other."

Cam walked around to the front of the wagon and pulled himself up next to the driver. "Lost, huh? Happens to the best of us."

Smirking despite himself, Clint climbed into his own saddle and looked around. The rest of the camp was all packed up and already starting to roll. "Anyone ever tell you that you're a pleasant man to talk to?"

"Nope," Cam replied after thinking for a second. "Can't say as they have."

"Good. Because they'd be lying their asses off."

The big man laughed as the wagon he was on lurched and started to move forward.

THIRTEEN

Jessup walked out of the small chapel in Allyn's Mill and took a deep, cleansing breath. The winter air chilled his lungs to an almost painful degree, but he kept sucking it in until his chest was swollen like a proud bird's. He felt good after going through the motions of the confessional and now he wanted to celebrate.

The first place he went was to his hotel room for a change of clothes. After all, if he was going to acquire any companionship for the rest of the evening, he had to look his best. In a matter of minutes, he was heading back down the stairs and out the hotel's front door, an even wider grin settling onto his youthful face.

The Mountainside Tavern was one of the finest saloons Jessup had seen in the area. Its owner was a European who did his best to dress up the place in all the trappings of a fine, upstanding drinking hall. There were paintings on the wall and a well-tuned piano, which was played by a real professional during peak business hours.

But, that wasn't to say that the place was as upstanding as its owner. The Mountainside Tavern was, despite all the fancy dressings and respectable airs, still a saloon at heart. And like any saloon that was worth its salt, it had potent liquor for its guests as well as plenty of women to entertain them. After the day he'd had, Jessup was in the mood for a taste of both.

He strolled into the saloon and shut the door behind him. As always, the piano player was playing some kind of somber classical number which hardly anyone in town recognized. The piece didn't have the kick of a Stephen Foster song, but it still managed to fill the room with a tranquil quality and kept the customers' voices down to a respectable level.

The large room was sectioned off into three parts. The first was an area of tables and chairs near the entrance. Some of these were covered with worn velvet and meant for playing cards, but mostly the tables were similar to those found in a restaurant, although in slightly better repair.

Along the back of the room was a narrow stage that was just big enough for a singer and a few accompanying dancers. Next to this was the piano player who was dressed in a smart, dark suit. His instrument was merely a straight-backed piano, but he played it as though he was in a concert hall.

At least, Jessup imagined that someone in a concert hall might carry himself in such a proud, almost pretentious manner.

Between these two areas was the pride of the room; a bar made from finely polished mahogany and carved with intricate designs of entwined vines and small flower buds. Even the brass rail running at the feet of the drinkers was as shiny as if it had only just been bought earlier that very day. The man behind the bar was dressed in a pressed shirt with his sleeves rolled down and buttoned at the wrist. He wasn't the owner, but he'd somehow managed to carry himself with the other man's grace and civility.

Jessup had only been to this saloon a couple of times before, but he loved it like a second home. There was just something about the Mountainside that made him feel better about himself. Perhaps it was the quiet music or the dark lighting and fine liquor. But mostly, he could relate to the place on a deeper level. Like him, the Mountainside was something common that had become something better.

Every town had its saloons, just like it had its killers. But occasionally one separated itself from the rest and placed itself above the rest. Jessup knew he was not only a gun for hire, but a killer extraordinaire. A true professional that deserved everything he got and earned every penny he made.

Setting these thoughts aside, he walked up to the bar and placed both hands flat upon the smooth wooden surface. "I'll have your finest malt whiskey," he said once the bartender looked his way.

"Of course," was all the other man said before turning and selecting a bottle from the rack built into the wall behind him.

Jessup turned and leaned his back against the edge of the bar, setting one heel onto the rail below. He took the glass that was handed to him and lifted it to his nose. The whiskey inside was potent, yet smooth to his senses. It slipped down his throat like it had been specially made for his personal tastes and gave his innards a sweet, warm glow.

Now that he'd gotten the first thing he was after, Jessup was ready to go after the next. To this end, he let his eyes roam over the other people that were inside the saloon, studying each prospect one by one. As always, the place was fairly crowded, but not packed to the rafters. There was a fair mix of gamblers, drinkers and those who were patiently waiting for the stage show to begin.

Among these, there were women of nearly every size, shape and color. There were even a pair of China dolls working their way through the crowd, one of which was pulled over by a man at one of the poker tables. She smiled widely and took her place on his lap, letting the other celestial beauty move on alone.

But Jessup wasn't interested in either of them for himself. Instead, he found a slender brunette who was standing behind a gambler who was in possession of an impressively large stack of chips. Her skin had a naturally golden hue which was accented beautifully by the dark, raven quality of her hair. She wore a dress which hugged her hips perfectly. The bodice was made from a shimmering, golden fabric which highlighted the curve of her pert, firm breasts.

The instant Jessup's eyes found her, he stopped looking for anyone else. Just like when he was lying in the dark staring down the barrel of his rifle, the killer let everything else in the world fade away until it was just a blur of unimportant shapes and a mumble of inconsequential sounds.

His target had been sighted. His sights were set. All that remained was for him to close in and pull the trigger.

FOURTEEN

Jessup took another sip of his drink, pulled his jacket straight and made his way across the room. Already, he could feel what it would be like to run his hands over her naked body. He knew her bare skin would be smooth and soft to the touch. Her voice would be equally sweet when it was calling his name.

When he was close enough to smell her hair, he put a hand on her shoulder and leaned in to whisper into her ear. "Hello there. My name is—"

The woman's eyes widened slightly and she smiled up at him. "I know who you are," she said in a voice that was slightly rough in an extremely sensual way. "I've seen you around town, haven't I?"

Jessup was surprised, but he didn't let it show. Instead, he shrugged and said, "Perhaps. If you're not busy here, I'd like to have you all to myself."

"All right," she said. Then, the woman leaned over to say her goodbyes to the gambler. Although the man at the table wasn't too happy to see her go, his spirits were picked up by the generous view he was given down the front of her dress. She giggled slightly when she felt the

56

gambler's hand slap her taut bottom and walked away next to her new companion.

Jessup led her to one of the few empty tables and pulled out her chair. Savoring the way she smiled at him as she sat, he pushed the chair in and walked around to sit in his own.

"My name is Eliza," she said while extending her hand.

Jessup took her hand in his and kissed it lightly. "Pleased to meet you, Eliza. I'm surprised you recognized me. Not many people do."

"Well, you might be surprised to hear this, but I do have a life outside of this place."

"I'm sure. In fact, I was just about to ask you if you'd like to leave this place."

"Excuse me?"

Jessup took hold of her hands and drew her closer. "I'd like you to come to my room," he whispered. "And I want to make love to you. I want to take those clothes off of you and taste every last inch—"

She stopped him in mid-sentence with a jarring slap across the face. Eliza's hand moved so fast that even Jessup hadn't seen it coming. The impact sounded worse than it was and the sharp noise rang through the entire section of the saloon.

More shocked than angry, Jessup didn't move back so much as an inch. He reached up to touch the spot where her hand had landed and looked down at it as though he still couldn't believe what had just happened. "I don't understand," he said. "I thought you're a—"

"I may be a lot of things," she said, cutting him off once again. "But I am obviously *not* what you thought I was. I can't believe what you were about to say to me!"

Jessup sat back in his chair and looked around the room. Although the others in the saloon were used to the occasional outburst, there were still a few too many people looking in his direction. Reflexively, Jessup kept his face turned down so that most of him was covered by his hat and upturned collar.

"Leave," he hissed. "Right now."

Eliza was already on her feet. "My pleasure," she said. "And I'll try to forget this happened."

Watching her leave in silence, Jessup took a slow sip of his whiskey. "You do that," he whispered to himself. "But I sure won't forget. You can bet your life on that."

It was a matter of moments before the chair across from Jessup was once again occupied. He'd just taken his last sip of expensive liquor when he noticed that he was once again being watched. Once Eliza had made her departure, the rest of the saloon had had the good sense to get back to their own affairs. The outburst had been amusing, but not enough to keep their attention for more than a few seconds. Now, Jessup could feel another pair of eyes on him.

In his line of business, the professional killer had instincts that jangled like a row of pans being hit by a wild child with a wooden spoon. And those instincts went off especially loud when he thought that someone was watching him. Looking up, Jessup immediately picked out the one who'd been staring. His hand had already drifted down to the spare pistol he kept hidden beneath his waistband.

The eyes that had been raising the hairs on the back of his neck belonged to a young girl who looked to be somewhere between nineteen and twenty-two years old. Her long brown hair was straight and glistened with the natural sheen of youth. She stood near the bar with her hip cocked to one side, her body wrapped in a dress that looked like one piece of material which had been wound around her body starting at her small, rounded breasts and stopping just below the sweet curve of her buttocks. From there, a lacy skirt fell down past her knees. A pair of high-heeled leather boots kept the rest of her wrapped up nice and tight.

When she saw that she'd been spotted, the girl turned her dark brown eyes away for just a moment before glancing back up. The move looked practiced, but was still extremely effective.

Jessup pointed a finger at her, turned his hand palm up and then hooked that same finger toward himself. No sooner had he completed the motion than he saw the young girl start walking toward his table. He made a different motion toward the bartender and sent for a refill of his drink, which arrived at roughly the same time as the girl.

He did so love the Mountainside Tavern.

The girl stood at his table and looked down at him with wide, luscious eyes. Her lips were full and pouting, glistening with the slightest hint of moisture. "My name's Sadie."

"Pleased to meet you Sadie," Jessup said with a nod. He accepted the fresh drink from the server and shooed the barkeep away. "Would you like to sit down?"

Sadie lowered herself into a chair and leaned forward to rest her elbows on top of the table. "I couldn't help but overhear you talking to Eliza."

"I'm sure the entire place heard that."

"Well, I think she was a fool to let someone like you go."

"Do you, now?"

She nodded, keeping her eyes locked on him. "In fact, I've been watching you ever since you came in here. Whatever you'd like to say to me . . . I'd listen."

"And what about after I'm done talking?"

"That's when things usually get interesting."

Jessup looked at the girl who was all but throwing herself at his feet. Although she didn't have the same spark that had attracted him to Eliza, there was something about her which stirred something inside of him. Her body was attractive enough and he was certain she knew her way around a bedroom, but there was something else. It was something on a more basic level than mere sex.

She looked at him like she thought she could take him for every penny in his pocket. After seeing the way he'd been treated by Eliza, the younger girl probably figured she could come on to him and appeal to his broken ego, using that as her way to wheedle in closer to the bottom of his pockets.

She had the look of a predator, much like many of the other more ambitious saloon girls. Jessup could respect that. And the more he thought about the look on her face once she realized that she'd been the one ensnared in a predator's trap, the more Jessup couldn't wait to get her alone.

"Would you like to go somewhere more private?" she asked.

Jessup put just the right amount of eagerness into his smile to make the girl's eyes shine hungrily. "Oh yes. More than anything."

FIFTEEN

Clint rode Eclipse right alongside the wagon that Cam had chosen and kept pace with the vehicle as it made its way toward the trail which led to Allyn's Mill. Despite the fact that they'd buried one of their own before heading out, the tension among the men seemed to have dropped significantly. In fact, they all seemed downright relaxed as they let the animals pull the wagons at their own pace.

The rumble of the wagon wheels churned through the air, mixing with the ever-present whistle of the wind. Even though the sun was on full display in the cloudless sky, none of its heat seemed to make it down to earth. Cold still hung like an invisible fog, which dug icy claws beneath everyone's coats and turned their breath into wispy steam.

"I'm still here," Clint said once the small caravan found its way back to the main trail. "Are you going to answer my question or should I just mark this day off as an unsolved mystery?"

Cam shifted in his seat. He'd pulled a rifle out from beneath the uncomfortable bench and was checking to make sure it was loaded when he started talking. "I know

61

you mostly by reputation, Adams. You ever do much work with the law?"

"Some. Why?"

"You ever seen the way a sheriff acts when one of his own gets killed? They pull together posses for a living, but when it gets personal, that's a whole other story."

Clint nodded. "True enough. Is that what you and these men are? A posse?"

Cam chuckled slightly. It was just enough to shake his upper body a few times beneath his layers of fur. "We ain't the law, but we are a kind of posse. And we're that kind of posse that takes its job real personal, if you know what I mean."

"I see. You've already had some of your own get killed by this man you're after."

Cam's eyes glossed over for a minute. He stared at Clint without actually seeing him. It was as though he wasn't seeing anything at all besides whatever visions played out inside his mind. He looked vaguely sad . . . a little angry . . . but mostly, he looked haunted.

"How many?" Clint asked.

Shaking his visions away, Cam focused in on his surroundings. "There's ten of us now." He twitched as though he'd been stung by a bee. "Make that nine. When all of this started, there were twenty of us that got together to hunt this piece of shit down. Twenty." When he repeated the number, Cam said it mostly to himself as though he could hardly believe it. "To answer that question that's been bothering you so much, that's what all of this is about. We're on a manhunt and it won't be over until we have that killer's filthy carcass skinned and nailed to the side of a barn."

"If you're not the law, then who are you?" Clint asked.

"We're a group of concerned citizens." The reply came out of Cam's mouth like a line that had been written for him in a script. It was spoken like a knee-jerk response and didn't require any thought whatsoever. The big man's normal tone came back, however, when he turned to give Clint a knowing look. "But I'm sure you know what that means even better than some of the law around here."

Nodding, Clint said, "Vigilantes."

Cam tapped the side of his nose and nodded slowly. "That's right, Mister Adams. And we'll get our man . . . even if we have to pick up some more help along the way."

"I hope you don't mind me saying, but you might want to reconsider this whole thing. Especially since you've already lost so many men."

"It's too late for that."

"Why? What did this killer do? Who the hell is he?"

"His name is Jessup. We don't rightly know if that's his first or last name. Hell, we don't even know if that's his real name at all. But what we do know is that he's a cold-blooded murderer who deserves to die a thousand times over. And even then, he still owes the devil to pay back for what he's done."

Clint paused for a second to let what he'd heard settle into his mind a bit longer. There was something familiar, which teased him at the edge of his mind like a voice that was close enough to hear, yet too far away to understand. He knew he'd heard that name before, but still he couldn't quite put his finger on anything more than that.

"Jessup," Clint said softly, hoping that hearing the name again would shake something else loose inside his head. "Jessup. Wasn't he wanted down in Louisiana for killing a judge?"

Cam nodded solemnly. "That was his first. He brags about that one because even though the law put a price on for murder, they weren't able to stop him from coming back to kill that judge's family and friends."

Clint stared at the other man in disbelief. He'd heard about the judge's death, but not anything else regarding the case. There were way too many criminals prowling about for him to keep track of them all. "Why would he do something like that?"

"He said it was to teach the world a lesson," Cam replied. "He said that the judge had no business tarnishing Jessup's good name and that his own death wouldn't cover the price. So Jessup took the judge's kin to square the bill. At least . . . that's the way he tells it."

"The way who tells it? Jessup?"

"That's right."

"So you know him? You've talked to him?"

That haunted look came back into Cam's eyes and he turned to glare straight ahead at the trail in front of him. "I talked to him all right. And I can still hear that son of a bitch's voice if I think about it. I hear it in my nightmares every night since this posse was formed up."

"So if you could have a conversation with this killer you're after, how come you couldn't have taken him in right then?" Clint asked.

"Because at the time we weren't after him, Mister Adams. At the time . . . we were riding with him."

SIXTEEN

Jessup held the door of his motel room open and watched as Sadie walked in ahead of him. Every move she made was designed to seduce and entice him. Every step she took was a flow of sensuous motion. Her hips swayed back and forth as her skirt hugged her body like a pair of lover's hands. Her heels clicked against the floorboards in a steady rhythm which carried her through the doorway and over to the side of his bed.

When she turned, Sadie ran her fingers through her hair, arching her back to thrust her breasts out provocatively. The dim flicker of the lantern threw a shadow over her which accentuated the nipples, which had already become hard beneath her bodice.

Without taking his eyes off of her, Jessup closed the door and fit the latch into place. The lock fell into position with a sharp metallic *click*.

"It's cold in here," she said, while running the palms of her hands over her sides and down to her hips. "You want me to start a fire?"

Eyeing her intently, Jessup said, "You keep doing that and we won't need any fire. I'll be plenty warm."

Sadie smiled and closed her eyes. She kept moving her

hands over her body, slowly writhing as if to some song that only she could hear. Her hands wandered up and down over her hips, drifting up to her breasts where they lingered as she gently squeezed and drew in a sharp, excited breath.

Watching all of this without making a sound, Jessup moved away from the door and to a chair which was positioned against the wall across from the foot of the bed. He lowered himself down and crossed his legs, folding his hands on top of his knee.

Moving like the expert showgirl she was, Sadie made sure that she was always in his line of sight. Her body drifted over the floor as she walked toward the bed, her hands never breaking contact with her own curves. She stood in front of him and swished her hips back and forth while peeling down the top of her dress to expose her smooth, naked skin.

Leaning forward, she tugged on the bodice until her erect nipples appeared over the top of the fabric. Sadie gave him an alluring smile while she lifted one of her fingers to her mouth and rubbed it along the edge of her lip. She let out a soft moan as she opened her mouth, allowing the tip of her tongue to emerge just long enough to moisten the end of her finger. Once that was done, she lowered her eyes to look at her bare breasts and rubbed her wet finger on the very tip of her nipple.

Jessup's breath caught in his throat as he watched the display. The flickering light of the room's single lantern accentuated every detail of the young woman's body, bathing it in warm light and velvety shadow. He could see her nipples growing smaller and taut as she pinched them between her moist fingers and rolled the pink nubs while purring softly.

She was moving closer to him now and before Jessup had a chance to catch his own breath, Sadie was straddling his leg. Jessup didn't resist one bit as Sadie un-crossed his legs by pushing aside one knee. And once she'd hiked up her skirt, she was able to straddle him enough so that she could grind her crotch against him while working her way closer to his waist.

Swallowing hard, Jessup reached out with both hands and placed his palms onto her naked legs. He moved up from there until he could slide his fingers beneath the material of her skirt. Sadie's clothes were already tight against her body, so when she felt his touch drifting closer up her thighs, she spread her legs open just enough to force the bottom of her skirt farther up.

Jessup's eyes drifted over the younger woman's body, savoring the way her clothes had been pushed aside one way and pulled another to expose her. As he shifted his gaze to her eyes, he could see that she was looking down at herself as well, enjoying her own nakedness almost as much as he.

At that moment, his fingers had wandered up between her legs and he could feel the warm wetness of her vagina. The girl's juices made her slick and soft. The instant he slipped a fingertip inside, the juice from her pussy trickled over his hand like a teardrop running down her leg. Rather than push farther inside, he moved his finger up until he could touch the delicate nub that was her clitoris.

Sadie's eyes clenched shut and she ground slowly against him. An excited little moan slipped out as her lips parted in a smile. She still wasn't looking at him. Instead, she seemed to be lost in her own world of pleasure and when Jessup started massaging her clit with his thumb, she bit down on her lower lip and moaned a little louder.

SEVENTEEN

Jessup's erection was so intense that it was almost becoming painful. No sooner had he started to squirm in his seat, before Sadie was reaching down to pull open his pants and stroke his cock between her strong, slender fingers.

First, Sadie hooked one leg around Jessup's lower body and clenched him tight. The other leg followed and she quickly locked her ankles at the small of his back to support herself as she scooted back to perch on his knees while tugging his pants down as far as she could. Although their position kept her from undressing him completely, she was able to get his erect penis freed from his clothing with enough room to allow her hands to slip between his legs and start massaging vigorously.

Jessup could hardly control himself once he felt Sadie's hands working up and down his shaft. She knew just when to squeeze and just when to keep still. She almost knew his body better than he did himself and she still had the presence of mind to shift her hips in a way that guided his own hand so that she could get just as much pleasure as she was giving him. His body seemed to be working purely off of instinct and when he gave in to it, Sadie responded in kind.

Both of their voices filled the room with constant, insistent grunts and moans. The instant Jessup took his fingers out of her, he felt Sadie shift her weight forward so that she could press her slit against the base of his cock. As much as Jessup wanted to be inside of her, he had to take a moment to just sit back and enjoy the feel of the slick lips between her legs as they rubbed up and down against his column of flesh.

Unable to wait another moment, Jessup reached around with both hands to cup her round little backside and pull her closer. Sadie held on to the back of the chair with both hands to steady herself as she moved along with him and lowered herself onto his rigid penis. Her legs were spread open so wide that he slid in easily and once she'd lowered herself down, she was sitting in his lap and leaning back to give him an enticing view of her small, naked breasts.

Feeling Jessup's hands guiding her, she strained with every muscle in her body to ride up and down on his cock. She pulled with her legs and pushed with her arms, baring her teeth as a thin layer of sweat began to form on her skin. Tiny drops trickled between her little breasts and her muscles pulsed beneath her flesh as she rode him hard enough to knock the back of the chair against the wall.

Jessup kept his hands on her backside, guiding her as she bounced up and down in his lap. Every time he let her come down, he pushed up with his hips so he could drive himself as deeply as possible between her legs. The sensations she was giving to him were so fantastic that he thought the room was spinning around him in slow circles.

Finally, when she reached the uppermost point of her bounce, Sadie stopped so that only the tip of his penis was still inside of her. Taking a slow, deep breath, she looked down at him and smiled while gripping him tightly between her legs.

Moving his hands to the small of her back, Jessup supported her weight as she leaned back, displaying her body proudly as he thrust inside of her once more. This time, he was the one in control and he drove inside of her relentlessly until he could feel their hips coming together in a hammering rhythm.

Jessup kept up his pace until he could hear Sadie's voice rising up into a passionate scream. Her pussy was clenched tightly around him now and she reached out to grab hold of his forearms for support. She thrust her hips back and forth until an orgasm caused her muscles to clench and her nails to dig deeply into his flesh.

It only took a few more thrusts before Jessup was about to climax and when he did he pounded inside her as deeply as he could and held that position until the last wave of pleasure had worked its way through his twitching body.

Using every last bit of strength he could muster, Jessup sat upright and started scooting to the edge of his seat. The girl on his lap dropped forward lazily and put her head on his shoulder. Realizing that he was trying to get up, Sadie locked her legs tightly around him, which sent ripples of pleasure through her overly sensitive body.

She nibbled on his neck and kissed his skin as Jessup lifted both of them up and off the chair. His hands held on to her trim buttocks to keep her right where she was as he took a few steps forward and set her down onto the bed. Reluctantly, Sadie released her grip on him as she was lowered onto the mattress. But she still didn't unlock her legs completely.

Even though he knew she was only trying to be playful, Jessup fought to get away from her. Eventually, he had to reach around and pull her legs from where they were locked around him.

"That was great," she said with a satisfied smirk. "If you want to do it again, I might not even charge you."

"Really?" Jessup said sarcastically. "That's real nice of you."

Sadie moved so that she could sit up with her back resting against the headboard. "Trust me ... I'm much better than that stuck-up whore you were talking to before."

Jessup's eyes flared with fleeting rage, which quickly subsided as he stepped forward. "You're ... you're right."

"Damn right I am." And with that, Sadie hopped off the bed and started tugging her clothes back into place.

"Where do you think you're going?" Jessup asked.

Sadie didn't even look at him. "To get a bath. You can come with me if you want, but it'll cost you extra."

Jessup's hand went for the pistol which was strapped to his ankle. After snatching the two-shot gun from its holster, he pulled his pants on and buckled up. His eyes were still on Sadie as she fussed with the line of her skirt and worked her fingers through her hair. There was something about the girl that made Jessup feel ... anxious.

Maybe it was how young she looked or maybe it was the way she talked. When she looked at him, she seemed sweet and sexy. But when she opened her mouth, she became a dirty whore. Even the sounds she'd made during sex had been almost feral grunts rather than passionate moans. And the more he thought about her in those terms, the more he wanted to let his darker instincts take over.

Her body had been so wet. So sweaty. To Jessup, that was only a prelude to how slick her blood would be as it ran over her skin. He could still feel her body twitching on top of him, much like the way a fresh kill twitched as it still tried to carry on with its life.

Jessup's hand tightened around his gun and he took a step closer to the girl who still had her back to him. She was talking about something or other; either about the money she was owed or trying to convince him to give her some more.

He could hear her saying things that made him excited, but not as excited as he would be if he allowed himself to pull that trigger. In his younger days, Jessup might have just put the little gun against Sadie's head and blown her brains onto the bed and wall of the hotel room. But that wasn't the way Jessup worked anymore. And he wasn't quite ready to leave Allyn's Mill just yet.

That last fact, more than anything else, was what saved the young woman's life.

"So what do you think?" she asked while turning around on the balls of her feet and fixing him with the same look that had worked on so many other men. "Am I going to see you later?"

Jessup had already stashed the gun behind his back and plastered on a convincing look of his own. "Of course you will."

EIGHTEEN

"So let me get this straight," Clint said. "You and all these men used to ride with Jessup. And yet now you're hunting him down?"

"Yep," Cam said, nodding.

"And you don't even know his whole name?"

Shaking his head slowly, Cam said, "Nope."

The caravan was still moving slowly, taking its own sweet time in getting to the nearby town of Allyn's Mill. Once the sun had started its descent toward the horizon, the air took on an extra added chill which was like an extra set of teeth in addition to the wintry fangs that had been gnawing at them all day long.

In the distance, the first signs of the town could be seen in the form of several strands of black smoke rising up into the sky. The outline of buildings came soon after that, but the town still seemed far away. Clint barely noticed any of those things, however, since he was still involved with his conversation with Cam. Unfortunately, he hadn't heard anything to make him feel much better than he had since he'd first met up with the group of men.

"Well that's just great. I'm starting to think that tagging along with this bunch wasn't such a great idea after all."

"You're free to leave any time you want. But I don't mind telling you that everyone here would appreciate it if you stayed."

"And why should I?" Clint asked. "If you used to ride with this killer, then that means you were killers yourselves. Don't even bother telling me that you were all saints at the time and Jessup just went bad. I've been around too long to believe that one."

"Oh I wasn't about to say anything of the sort. None of us that rode with him were anything close to saints. In fact, we made our living stealing and killing, but mostly the first and only a bit of the second."

Although Clint was getting more than a little annoyed with the turn the conversation had taken, he figured he'd heard this much and might as well hear the rest. "So what happened to change things around?"

"Actually, only about half of the men you see here were with us in the old days." Pointing to the man who rode at the front of the line, Cam explained, "Gordon there found us all and brought us together as a group."

"Group? Don't you mean a gang?"

Cam's face twisted slightly and he shook his head. "I don't think so. We weren't together long enough to be a real gang. Hell, the whole idea was just to get together, pull a few jobs that were big enough for us all to retire and then we'd split up. Gordon didn't even want us to know each other by our proper names so once the jobs were done, there wouldn't be no way for any one of us to cause any trouble for the others."

Clint nodded as the details began to come together inside his head. He might not have agreed with what Cam had done in the past, but it was sure nice to finally have some things start making sense. "So that's why you don't know Jessup's whole name."

"You got it. And he don't know ours."

"I'm no robber, but that sounds like a good setup. What went wrong?"

"Jessup went wrong, that's what," Cam said distastefully. "He started killing when it wasn't needed and kept right on killing even after we'd be done with a job." Turning to look at Clint, his eyes took on that haunted quality once again. For such a big, imposing figure, it was a little disconcerting to see him so spooked when he was just talking about this man they were after. "You ever seen a mad dog, Adams?"

"Yeah. I've seen some on four legs as well as the ones on two. Neither one of them are very good to have around."

Amused with that, Cam said, "No they're not. You are certainly right about that. I thought I'd seen my share of mad dogs. Anyone that rides with any unsavory sorts usually runs across a few here and there. The thing about mad dogs is that they tend to take care of themselves. Either they bite off more than they can chew or they kill so much that the rest of the dogs they run with have no choice but to put them down.

"Jessup walked into this railroad office we were going to rob. A payroll was set to come through and he was to take care of the clerk and any guards that were posted inside. You see, we gave him that job because we knew he didn't mind the rough jobs.

"Anyway . . . we heard the shots and then went through with the job. The whole thing took less than a few minutes because Gordon is hell and Jesus with planning those things. We all rode out separately and were to meet up outside of town later that day. A few hours go by and we all start trickling in one by one until we're all at the spot except for Jessup. We waited another hour or two before me and Gordon rode back to see what had happened."

The haunted air that had been hanging around Cam's head dissipated the more he spoke. It seemed as though

the demons he'd been carrying around with him had become familiar company by now. "When we got back, we
found Jessup right where we'd left him. He was still in
the railroad office . . . with the clerk . . . and three guards.
Jessup was the only man who was still in one piece.

"There were . . . parts lying scattered all around that
room. And the blood . . . there was more of it there than
I'd ever seen in one place before. That's coming from a
hunter, Mister Adams. I've slaughtered buffalo and used
to spend days covered in blood. When I think about that
office . . . it turns my stomach. And you know what the
worst part of it was?"

Clint shook his head.

"They were still alive. Every last one of 'em was still
alive." Cam took a deep breath and stared straight ahead.
When he spoke this time, his voice was lighter. More
detached. "Jessup cut off fingers and feet. It looked like
he just cut off pieces of meat on a few of them. He knew
what he was doing. He had to. With all he did to them
people, it took extra effort to keep them alive. Once we
bust in there and found him, I remember he looked up at
me . . . his face covered in blood . . . and said he'd created
a masterpiece. Some kind of work of art."

"Jesus Christ," Clint said under his breath.

"He wasn't nowhere near that place, Mister Adams. In
fact, that was the day that I damn near stopped believing
that any kind of God could exist that would let a monster
like that roam his earth."

NINETEEN

"So after that, I can only guess that Jessup got worse," Clint said.

Cam spat on the ground as though he was getting rid of a piece of rotten meat. "Hell if I know. After that, we got out of that place and left Jessup behind. Gordon and I . . . we woke up in that office. We woke up to all the things we done and all the evil we committed. It's easy to be a thief after you convinced yourself that you ain't been doing nothing wrong. We pulled jobs and didn't kill a soul. But when we saw the blood in that room, we got a good look at what evil truly is."

Speaking in a strong, solid voice once again, Cam looked to Clint and said, "He was one of us. He might have been the mad dog, but we were all in the same pack. And none of us could live with ourselves after seeing that and knowing that all of that blood had been spilled because we put Jessup there at that place and time."

At first, Clint fought back the impulse to empathize with the confessed robber. But then he realized that Cam was already more sorry for what he'd done than any other man who was supposedly paying for his crimes in a cell, or even at the end of a rope. And there was something else to Cam's story that Clint wanted to hear. Until he heard something else to change his mind, he decided that Cam deserved to be heard. Even a blind man could see that he was still being punished for those days of lawlessness.

"You didn't kill those men," Clint said. And even though he hadn't been there to witness the deaths himself, he knew that to be true. He had too much faith in his instincts to start doubting them now and those instincts told him that Cam was no mad-dog killer. "If you hadn't been riding with him, Jessup would have killed somewhere else. You can't blame yourself for what someone else does."

"That worked for a while, Adams. But we don't know what Jessup might have done on his own. Without me or Gordon to pave the way, he might have been caught sooner. But it was too late by the time we found him in that office. He'd tasted blood and liked it. More than that, he'd had enough practice to become real good at killing."

"So what happened after that job?" Clint asked, genuinely interested in the other man's story.

"Like I said, me and Gordon woke up. We told Jessup he wasn't welcome with us anymore and that we'd kill him like the mad dog he was if'n we ever set eyes on him again. After that . . . we left. Me, Gordon and the rest of the boys left all the money we'd taken from that job where the law could find it and rode off."

"But that wasn't enough, was it?" Clint asked.

Cam laughed slightly even though he didn't have the slightest trace of humor in him at the moment. "No, that wasn't. But how did you know that?"

"Because if that was enough, your story would be over. And I've got a feeling you've still got some left to tell."

"Nothing gets by you, Adams. We'd put Jessup behind us, but none of us could say more than two words to each other as we rode across the country. It seemed like we couldn't get far enough away from what had happened. We were just going to hole up in the next state, but we had to keep going. We rode for weeks, but we still couldn't get the stink of blood out of our noses.

"Finally, we stopped riding and had a talk. All of us knew what was bothering us, but didn't know what to do about it. Jessup was still out there. We knew he'd kill again, just like we knew that we were to blame for making him into the man he was. And before you say anything, Adams," Cam said while glancing toward the man who rode beside him. "We *were* responsible. It's too late to shake that now."

Clint held up his hands as though he was at gunpoint. "Sorry to be so predictable."

"We knew what we had to do," Cam continued. "There was only one way for us to go on with our lives and not be chewed up for what happened. The only way for us to start our new lives was to clean up what was left of our old ones. We had to end what we started and to do that . . ."

It seemed that Cam was suddenly having trouble coming up with the words he needed. So Clint stepped in to pick up the slack. "To do that, you needed to take care of Jessup."

"That's right. We didn't even need to kill him. After what he'd done to those guards, we knew that any self-respecting vigilantes would put him down as soon as he got into custody. Since we didn't have the stomach for killing anymore, we set out to catch Jessup and hand him over to the law."

"I have to say, that's pretty admirable of you," Clint admitted. "I've known more than my share of outlaws who would've seen fit to part ways and head for the border."

"If we was smart, we would've done just that," Cam

said in a voice that was tainted with regret. "But we weren't very smart. Not by a long shot."

Clint looked away from the wagon next to him for the first time in what felt like hours. Since the line of horses and wagons were still moving so slowly, it seemed the town of Allyn's Mill was rolling toward them. Listening to the slight rumble of wooden wheels crunching over packed snow, Clint might have felt as though he and Eclipse were standing on a piece of loose earth sliding over an ice flow.

Bloody images from Cam's story were still fresh in his mind, making the chill in the air seem that much colder and the wind that much calmer. Although he was anxious to hear what Cam had to say next, Clint stopped himself before urging the other man to continue. There was something about the way he sat hunched over next to the wagon driver that made Cam look like he was fighting just to keep his head up.

It was more than fatigue that weighed him down. Rather, it was the pressure of so many bad memories, which pushed on the back of his neck like a giant's boot shoving his face into the dirt. When Cam was ready, he would talk again. So Clint waited for that moment instead of trying to help it along.

"We did go back for him," Cam said before too much longer. "And what happened once we caught up to him was something we could have never prepared for. Not in a hundred years."

TWENTY

It had only been a little over a year ago, but to Cam and the rest of his men who'd been there, it felt like a whole other lifetime. Along with Cam and Gordon, there were a dozen other men. All of them had worked on the jobs they'd pulled and not a one of them had a doubt in their mind as to the righteousness of their cause.

No matter how dead set they were against killing, each of the men in the group were going to rest easier once Jessup was dead. It didn't take much work for them to find the last member of their group. In fact, they hadn't had to find him at all.

Once they rode over the border into Louisiana, Jessup had found them.

It was autumn when they'd ridden across the state line. All along the way, they'd been asking their contacts and allies about where Jessup had gone and what he'd been doing. None of the people they'd approached wanted to talk. They might have known plenty about Jessup's whereabouts, but were too scared to say a word.

Cam and Gordon were leading the group, which consisted of their entire gang except for the one missing member they were hunting. Even though the men knew each other better than their own brothers, they were hesitant to say a word once they'd taken on their self-appointed task. And the fact that they weren't getting much help from anyone outside the group didn't hamper them in the least.

They didn't think they'd have a problem finding Jessup. On the contrary, they all felt a chill run through their bones the farther they rode. That chill was unmistakable. It told them they were getting closer to Jessup and none of the men thought to question the accuracy of their instincts.

Still heading south, they'd just crossed into a wide field full of reeds that swayed in the gentle wind like a thousand waving arms. The air was fragrant and warm on their faces, making them feel better than they had in days. And just when they were all starting to relax, the peaceful silence was broken by the unmistakable crack of gunfire.

The shot came from somewhere behind the riders. The bullet whipped through the air and creased the skull of one of the men in the back of the formation, knocking the hat from his head and causing all of them to draw their weapons and pull their horses around so they were facing the new threat.

"Over there," Gordon had said, pointing to a section of bushes and high weeds. "It came from there! Fan out and keep moving."

The men did as they were ordered and several of them started firing back toward the bushes. But they were firing blind and their shots riddled the surrounding area in a broad, scattered pattern. The only one of them to drop down from his saddle was Cam. Although not wearing the furs he would don in winter, he was still covered with ragged animal hides stitched together to form a suit of tanned skins which covered him from toe to shoulders.

Cam already resembled an Indian simply by the way he dressed. That resemblance only grew when he crouched down close to the ground and drew his weapons. In one hand, he held a pistol and in the other, he carried a small knife that was balanced for throwing.

"Don't waste your ammo," Cam scolded. "Not until you can see what you're shooting at, dammit!"

The return fire tapered off for a second or two, which was just long enough for the hidden shooter to let off another shot of his own. This time, however, he did not miss. Snapping back as though he'd been punched in the face, the same man who'd just lost his hat to the sniper toppled over backward, leaving several strings of blood hanging in his wake.

Cam was the first one over to the fallen man's side. He looked down and saw that a section of the man's skull had been clipped off by the passing bullet and blood was pouring from the wound. The man died while Cam watched, but the rest of the group had already chosen that moment to charge the bushes.

There were more shots coming from both sides. Having heard the sniper's weapon twice was enough for Cam to pick that distinctive sound out from all the rest. The men in his own group favored pistols and shotguns, which made it that much easier to recognize the sharper voice of a rifle.

Cam knew who was doing the shooting and he also knew that if they didn't put the sniper down quick, the entire group might just come to a very bad end. His face twisted into an angry snarl, Cam crouched down low and surged into the fray, reflexively shooting in the direction where the rifle shots had been coming from.

The fight was intense, yet extremely short and soon the gang was gathering on the edge of the clearing to reload and regroup. The first thing Cam noticed was that they were three members short.

TWENTY-ONE

"Did anyone get a look at who that was?" Cam asked.

"It was Jessup," Gordon replied. "I didn't have to see the son of a bitch to know that much."

As much as Cam didn't like to rely on such shaky conclusions, he couldn't help but agree with that one. "Where's the rest of the boys?"

Gordon was busy reloading his pistol, his eyes darting back and forth to search for any trace of their attacker. "Kyle's dead. He took one in the heart. What about John?"

Cam shook his head. Part of him was responding to the question, and the other part was trying to shake out the image of John lying on the ground with his head cracked open like an egg. "That only leaves Sanchez. Did he catch a bullet too?"

Gordon snapped the cylinder of his pistol shut with a flick of his wrist. "I don't know. But if he's still not here, then he's probably not about to show up."

One of the others had finally managed to catch his breath. But rather than using it to calm himself, the young man kept breathing faster and faster until panic began to infect him like a disease. "What the hell happened? Who was that? Was that Jessup? What the hell's wrong with him? Is he crazy?"

"Shut up," Gordon barked while fixing the young man with a fierce look. "Just shut yer mouth while I try to think of somethin'."

Cam lifted his nose to the wind and looked slowly about. "The shooting's stopped."

"Right," Gordon said. "So if you keep quiet, we might be able to hear footsteps or something that'll let us know where to aim."

With that, the entire group fell silent.

As if on cue, the sound of irregular footsteps came from the bushes and headed straight for the group of men. Every one of them lifted their weapons and aimed in that general direction. The combined tension inside of them was almost thick enough to see. It crackled over their skin like dry, desert lightning.

As one, all of the men sighted down the barrels of their weapons, waiting for the first opportunity they could find to put a bullet into whoever it was that had opened fire on them from out of nowhere. The footsteps kept coming until finally a figure stumbled into view.

Rushing in so fast, Sanchez nearly got himself pumped full of lead by his own friends. The Mexican was too shaken to notice how close he'd come, however, and kept rushing straight toward the group until he was within arm's reach of Gordon.

Taking hold of Sanchez by the front of his shirt, Gordon pulled the Mexican almost off his feet. "What're you tryin' to do?" he hissed. "Get yerself killed? Get down before you get yer fool head blown off."

"He's gone," Sanchez said in a wavering voice.

Cam leaned forward and stared directly into Sanchez's face. "Who's gone? Was it Jessup?"

Sanchez nodded. "He was waiting for me. He ... took a swing at me, but I think he missed." The Mexican

pointed toward the right side of his head. At first, it had
been hard to notice all of the blood there because his hair
was so dark and so thick. But when he turned to look
toward Cam, the light glistened off the wetness that mat-
ted his hair down against his scalp.

"What the . . . ?" Gordon whispered as he brushed aside
the Mexican's hair. His features immediately darkened
when he got a look at what had happened. "My God."

That's when Cam was able to get a look for himself.
The Mexican's ear was gone. There wasn't any shredded
skin hanging down or even a gaping wound. All that remained was a bloody hole.

"Was it . . . bitten off?" one of the other men asked.

Cam shook his head. "No. It's too neat to be a bite.
Looks like a knife wound. Probably a razor."

Sanchez was becoming more confused the longer he
listened to the other men. Reaching up to feel the side of
his head, he immediately winced in pain as soon as his
finger touched the spot where his ear had been. *"Madre
de dios!"*

"He was sliced so clean and so fast he barely even felt
it," Cam pointed out.

"Where was he?" Gordon asked in a voice that was
calm and commanding. "Is he coming back?"

Sanchez shook his head. Some of the color was drain-
ing from his face and he lowered himself into a sitting
position on the ground. "He took my goddamn ear. He's
loco!"

"He sure as hell is," Gordon said. "We'll get you fixed
up, but you got to tell us what you saw before he comes
to pick us off while we're sittin' here flappin' our gums."

TWENTY-TWO

After drawing in a few deep breaths, Sanchez managed to pull himself together so he could talk coherently. "He's not coming back. I saw him take off running."

"But that don't mean he won't circle around just as we let our—"

"I'm telling you," Sanchez interrupted. "He's not coming back. Not yet, anyway."

Since most of the men had been hoping to hear something like that anyway, they were willing to take the Mexican's word for gospel. Cam and Gordon, on the other hand, were much more wary.

"How do you know that?" Cam asked. "What happened when you found him?"

"He took a swing at . . ." Sanchez stopped short and had to struggle to keep from touching his fresh wound. "Then . . . he pointed a rifle at me and whispered in my ear."

"This was happenin' during all the shooting?" Gordon asked disbelievingly. "How'd he manage to pull that off with all the lead that was flying back and forth?"

"He didn't seem to care about that. All he cared about was keeping us low and jamming that rifle barrel under my chin. He told me that he knew we were after him. He said that he was waiting for us ever since we left him after the last job."

"Oh, he was upset about that, was he?" Gordon snarled. "He's got some nerve, that one."

But Cam didn't let himself get too angry at that moment. Instead, he tried to calm Sanchez down while some of the others fetched a flask of whiskey from one of their saddlebags. "Go on. What did he say after that?"

Blinking away another sharp twinge of pain, Sanchez stifled back a curse before continuing. "He said this was just the start and that he was going to hunt us down like cowardly rats 'cause that's all we are. And he said when he found us . . . it would make what he did to those guards look like nothing at all."

Suddenly, Gordon leapt to his feet and snapped back the hammer of his Smith and Wesson. "Where's John? If he let you go and killed two others, that means we're still missin' John."

The only one who didn't show any concern about the missing member of their group was Sanchez. Wheeling around to glare at the Mexican head-on, Gordon said, "You know, so tell me."

"John is *muerto*. He's dead. I saw the body." Swallowing hard, Sanchez forced himself to go on. "Jessup had the body with him. When he let me go, he told me to head here and not look back, but I did. I looked back and I saw Jessup dragging John's body."

"Dragging the body where?" Cam asked.

Sanchez didn't have an answer for that. He could barely shrug as his attention went back to the piece of him that had been sliced off his body by the madman who'd almost taken his life as well. "I wasn't next to die," the Mexican said in a vague, almost faraway voice.

Cam squinted at Sanchez as though he was trying to

see what was going on inside the other man. "What was that?"

For a moment, Sanchez looked as though he didn't even remember speaking. But then he blinked and nodded as the rest came back to him in a rush. "I heard him say that just before he let me go. He said I wasn't next to die, and that I would have to wait my turn just like the rest of you." Looking at each member of the group in turn, he said, "Jessup's loco. He'll hunt us down and kill us . . . no matter how long it'll take.

"I saw that in his eyes. He's *loco para la sangre*. Crazy for the blood," the Mexican said, translating his own words for the gringos. "Like an animal. He wants to kill us. Just like he did to those guards."

As the weight of those words sunk in, all of the men started to get spooked. Even Gordon and Cam weren't immune to the effect, but none of them allowed their discomfort to degenerate into total fear. There was too much that needed to be done for them to start getting scared. And if they let themselves slip just once, it would be a hard road to find their way back.

Cam busied himself with tending to Sanchez's wound the best he could. Gordon searched the area for any trace of Jessup, but didn't find anything except for a few rifle shell casings and a whole mess of blood. The rest of the men prepared to ride on. No matter how badly they might have wanted to go home, it was too late to turn back now.

TWENTY-THREE

They found John's body toward the end of the next day. True to his word, Jessup had mutilated the corpse almost beyond recognition. The only thing that had been left intact was half of his face and one of his legs. Everything else looked as though it had been forced through a meat grinder and poured into a man's clothes.

Cam had been acting as scout and had been the one to come across the body, which had been propped up like a scarecrow just off the trail they'd been riding. He told the others that the gunshot wound in John's head was older than the rest, but that was just to ease the others' minds.

In reality, Cam couldn't rightly say which wound came first and everyone else had been content to believe that Jessup had at least had the decency to kill his victim before carving him up.

What stuck in Cam's mind even more than the horrific wounds was what he'd found on John's forehead. There'd been three words dug into the dead man's skin. The sliced letters reminded Cam of notes carved into tree trunks once the bark had been stripped away.

Next to die.

Those three words, written in deep, red grooves in the

dead flesh stared back at Cam with more intensity than John's eyes, which were still open and glaring vacantly at the world. Knowing that Jessup was done with the body, Gordon buried John in the first clearing he could find along the side of the trail.

The rest of the men were glad to pay their respects at the gravesite. This was partly due to the fact that they'd been worrying about what could have been happening to John while he was in Jessup's company and now those worries had been put to rest. But there was still that part of each man which was glad to commit John to the earth simply so they could do their best to forget about him. After all, no matter how much they might mourn, having John out of sight made it easier to put him out of mind.

But the memory of his disfigured body didn't fade easily. And when they set off again, those three words that had been carved into his skin hung over all of their heads like the unspoken words of a devil.

Who would be next to die?

Would it be just one or every one of them?

Even though the group knew they could overpower the madman, they also knew for a fact that Jessup would take at least a few of them out before he was dead. Now that they'd seen the type of carnage that their quarry was capable of, they weren't too eager to put themselves in the line of fire.

Without saying much of anything to one another, the remaining members of the group set off once again into an uncertain future. Cam couldn't stop thinking about what they could do against a creature as depraved as Jessup. He could be anywhere, after all, and he could be doing anything.

As for Gordon . . . he spent his time enthralled in the hunt and planning silently to himself. Only once did Gordon ever admit what he'd been thinking about during all those long, quiet hours, and that was only to Cam himself.

"You don't want to know what I'm thinkin'," Gordon had said on the second night after they'd come across John's body.

Cam tended to their fire and stared into the flickering flames. "Of course, I do. Otherwise, I wouldn't have asked."

After a slight pause, Gordon spat something onto the ground near his feet and said, "I been thinkin' of a way to hurt Jessup. He needs to be punished, Cam. But after seein' what he done . . . and knowin' that he likes doin' it . . . I'll be damned if I can think of a way to hurt him."

"I know what you mean. It's kind of like trying to think of a way to hurt the devil, himself. Anything we might do just seems to pale in comparison to what he's already used to. Just like we can't make a fire that's hotter than it is in hell."

Gordon actually smiled at that. "That's why I like talkin' to you. It's never boring."

Ignoring the compliment, Cam let another few moments pass by before asking, "So what did you come up with?"

"Nothing," Gordon spat. "Not one damn thing."

"Actually, that's not too bad."

"How do you figure? Jessup needs something worse than a bullet to pay for what he's done and I can't come up with a goddamned thing."

"That's not what I meant," Cam said simply. "What I meant was that it's not a bad thing that you can't think of such terrible things as well as Jessup. If you'd already come up with something fitting for that monster, I might've started to worry about you."

Gordon chewed on that for a bit before he finally turned to look at Cam head-on. When he did, he was wearing a thin smile on his face. "Right there. That's the other reason I like talkin' to you."

TWENTY-FOUR

The next day, just as the men's spirits had started to rise from the ashes that Jessup had sent them, another shot broke the tranquil silence that had been swirling in the air.

Unlike the last time, the entire group had been prepared for the worst and didn't break into immediate panic. Instead, they looked carefully around to find where the shot might have come from. Each one of the men pressed their senses to their limits so they wouldn't miss a single hint.

"Over there!" Gordon said in a voice laced with hopeful excitement. "He fired from over there. I can still see the smoke!"

He was pointing to a small pile of boulders that was just big enough to keep one man concealed so long as he was lying on his stomach. The others broke formation in the precise way they'd planned and started to circle around in an attempt to flank their target.

All of them except for one.

One of the men, a young southerner they'd called Eagle, rocked slowly back and forth in his saddle. A wide-eyed, confused look was painted on his face. Just as Cam looked over to see what was the matter with him, Eagle blinked once and let out a breath. A trickle of blood ran down from beneath his hat.

Before Cam could say a word, Eagle dropped off his horse and was dead before he hit the ground. That single shot which had been fired dug a hole straight through the young man's head, answering the question that had been on all of their minds ever since they'd seen the words cut into John's flesh.

Gordon barked out orders as his eyes became slits of angry fire. He directed the others like they were soldiers in a war and not one of them proved to be a disappointment.

It was too late for any of the men to be scared. Even Sanchez, who carried the worst scar out of any of the survivors, choked back his fear and took up his weapon. He used his pain the way a steam engine used coal. It drove him and the others faster down the road they'd been forced upon.

The men scrambled, but they were already too late. Somehow, Jessup had managed to get away. Cam figured that the madman had taken off as soon as he'd squeezed the trigger on that rifle of his. More than likely, Jessup hadn't even taken the time to make sure he'd hit his mark or not.

Now, more than ever, Cam felt like a hapless bird that was being chased down by an expert hunter. It didn't matter what he did or what he thought. There was simply no way to change the way things were headed.

Every step he took could have been keeping him alive or he might just be running in the way he'd been herded.

All of these notions flew through Cam's mind in the space of a heartbeat. And in the end, he only had one choice. He could give up or keep on with his own hunt.

Who was next to die?

At that time, it seemed that only Jessup knew for sure.

TWENTY-FIVE

Clint listened to the story as Eclipse carried him down the trail next to Cam's wagon. The town of Allyn's Mill loomed ahead of them and they were close enough to hear voices coming from one of the saloons by the time Clint took a moment to check on their progress. Even though a warm fire and hot meal were only a couple yards away, he still couldn't get himself to break away from the small caravan.

"So how many of your men did Jessup kill that time?" Clint asked.

Cam hadn't looked up more than once or twice since he'd started telling his story. Now that he was almost finished, he lifted his gaze so that it met Clint's. The haunted look was still there, but it had faded over the last hour, mostly due to the cold in the air and the weariness in his bones. "Just one. He didn't get ahold of Eagle's body, though. I made sure of that."

"And Jessup got away? Even after shooting one of your men right out from under your noses? And even when you knew something like that would be coming?"

"We all know death is coming, Adams. That don't make you any more ready when it finally arrives." Cam

paused and shifted the gun in his hands while preparing
to climb down once the wagon came to a stop. "Jessup
ain't like anything I ever seen before. We were ready for
the worst, but we just didn't have a notion how bad that
was gonna be.

"He would pick us off one at a time. I think he was
saving me and Gordon for last because we were the lead-
ers of the group. Still are, I guess. Anyway, we did a good
job of chasing him and learned from our mistakes. Whenever we'd track him down, though, he would slip away.
And if we followed too close, he'd gun our men down."

"And this has been going on for a year?" Clint asked.

Nodding, Cam said, "On and off. Me, Gordon and the
rest do jobs here and there to keep us in money, but nothing illegal. Mostly bounty hunting, since manhunting is
all we're good at anymore. And when one of us gets
dropped, we carry the bodies with us and bury them only
when we know Jessup ain't nowhere around."

"So how do you expect to find him?"

"He may be wild and bloodthirsty, but Jessup's like any
other animal. He'll get tired and he'll make a mistake.
When he does, we'll be there. Until then, we keep running him from place to place, hopefully flushing him out
before he gets a chance to hurt anyone. After what we
started . . . it's the least we can do."

After listening to Cam's story for the better portion of
the ride into town, Clint felt like he had a good understanding of what had driven these men to dedicate their
lives to this hunt. And since he'd seen part of their con-
frontation with his own eyes, he was fairly certain that at
least some of what he'd been told was actually true.

But in his experience, "some" only left room for a
whole lot of uncertainty. Whether it be on purpose or not,
that uncertainty could put any man into a world of hurt
if he didn't bother questioning what he'd heard. Clint

wasn't about to buy into the story right away, but he also wasn't about to write it off completely.

Cam looked too tired to lie convincingly for so long. But that didn't mean that his story wasn't tainted just because it had been told from only one point of view. Clint decided that he needed a bit more proof before he could help the group with their task. After all, even if a part of the story was based in fact, those were some awful disturbing facts.

Not waiting to see what Clint had to say, Cam climbed down from the wagon as soon as it came to a stop. He reached for the sky, stretching his aching back and stomping his cramped feet on the hard earth. "Well, this is where we stop for the night. I appreciate the company, Adams."

"You're just going to park out front here and get some sleep?" Clint asked. "I hate to question your judgment, but aren't you a bit concerned that Jessup is still nearby?"

"Of course he's nearby," Cam said in an exhausted voice. "He's always nearby. But he's hit us once today and gotten the blood he wanted. Even a vicious animal still has his patterns and Jessup's is to wait, kill, and then wait some more."

"Are you willing to bet all of your lives on that?"

Pulling down a satchel with his own personal gear in it, Cam replied, "We've been doing that for a long time now. Why stop here?" Hefting the satchel under his arm, Cam turned and waved over his shoulder. "Take care of yourself, Adams."

Clint watched the big man stride into a small hotel just across the street. Gordon was already through the door and all but one of the men filtered slowly inside as well. They left that one man to stay with the wagons. Glancing up toward the last remaining member of the group that he could see, Clint found that it was Sanchez who'd been left behind.

"That was a hell of a story," Clint said.

In response, the Mexican simply nodded. That gesture seemed to sap a great deal of what little energy he had left. "It sure is. But you'd best believe it all the same." And with that, Sanchez removed his hat and pulled the collar of his coat down to reveal the side of his head. In the place where his ear should have been, there was nothing but a gnarled hole surrounded by rough, scarred flesh. It was painful even to look at, but Clint managed to keep from reacting to the gruesome sight.

"You should really go to the law," Clint offered. "I know some people who would help you find Jessup. I mean . . . with what you already know, they could even use some of your men to—"

"It ain't their problem," Sanchez interrupted. "It's ours. Calling in the law would only get some more good men killed." His eyes wandering to the wagon where the body of Jessup's latest victim had been stored, Sanchez added, "There's been too much of that already."

Watching as the haunted shadow crept over Sanchez's face just as it had done Cam's, Clint had an easier time believing that a group of admitted outlaws really could change their ways. Gordon's men had chosen a hard, treacherous road, of that Clint was certain.

They seemed to be good men. Clint's gut told him that.

But did Clint believe in them enough to lend his gun to their hunt? Since that would mean following the men into a dark corner of hell, Clint decided to wait just a bit longer.

TWENTY-SIX

Eliza Morrow loved the cold.

As she stepped out of the Mountainside Tavern, she pulled her wool wrap around her just a bit tighter and lifted her face to accept the chill, winter breeze. It made her skin tingle and the tip of her nose go numb, but she still loved the freshness that could only be found in the cold.

She always thought that things were cleaner in the cold. After all, food stayed fresher in cold places and things didn't get a chance to assault the senses like they did in the summertime. Heat made things rot. Heat made people sweat. Heat made everything stink and swelter. And if anyone knew about sweaty, stinking things, it was a girl who made a living in Eliza's line of work.

Glancing down the street, her eyes were immediately drawn to a line of wagons that had been parked in front of the hotel. Eliza knew it wouldn't be long before she got a chance to meet some of those men, but that would have to wait until tomorrow. Right now, all she wanted to do was walk home in the refreshing cold and put the Mountainside Tavern behind her.

Just as Eliza was concentrating on that task, the silence

she'd been enjoying was suddenly shattered by an excited, almost screeching voice coming from the saloon.

"Eliza!" the voice shouted. "Eliza, over here."

Not more than two buildings away from the Mountainside, Eliza still thought she could get away with ignoring whoever was calling her until she could duck into an alley or around a corner. For a moment, she thought she'd been able to escape the familiar voice. But those hopes were dashed when she heard the voice again. This time, it came from a few feet behind her.

"You walk so fast, Eliza. I swear you were trying to run away from me."

Eliza stopped and turned around slowly. By the time she was facing the other woman, she'd managed to plaster on a semi-convincing smile. "Hello Sadie. I guess I didn't hear you."

The younger girl's hair was a tussled mess and her clothes had the rumpled look of having just been hastily thrown over her body. "Well I was screaming loud enough to wake the dead. And I nearly fell flat on my face from running to catch up with you."

"Sorry about that. What did you want?"

"Just to walk home with you. We only live across the street from each other and yet I feel like I hardly ever get to see you."

Actually, that was a result of Eliza's careful planning and strategic movements in and out of her door. Only through such drastic efforts did she get a moment's peace from the younger woman who never seemed to get the hint that her grating presence wasn't always welcome. That was probably because Sadie was used to getting attention heaped on her by her customers at the saloon. But Eliza wasn't alone in her dislike for the slender girl. The fact that Sadie never hesitated to pounce on someone else's customer had earned her no small amount of malice from the rest of the working girls.

Eliza's first impulse was the same as any other time she saw Sadie coming. But since she couldn't get away cleanly at the moment, she figured she might as well be polite and try to get away. But there was something different this time. There was a look in the younger woman's eyes that made Eliza pause before turning away.

"Are you all right, Sadie?"

"Of . . . of course. Why?"

"I don't know. You look . . . frightened. Did one of those men do something to scare you?"

Suddenly conscious of her appearance, Sadie fussed with her hair and checked to make sure that her dress had been fastened properly. "He didn't hurt me or anything, but . . ." She smiled uncomfortably and shifted on her feet. "I'm probably just tired, is all. This damn cold makes me feel strange sometimes. It gets so dark so early in the day."

"I know," Eliza said fondly. Going against every one of her reflexes regarding the other woman, Eliza reached out to put an arm around her shoulder. "Come on. You're shaking. And it doesn't look like the kind of shaking someone does just because it's cold outside. Why don't you come with me and I can fix you some tea?"

For the first time since she'd caught up to Eliza, Sadie smiled warmly and seemed to relax. "Thank you," she said with genuine affection. "I'd really like that."

As she started walking, Sadie moved in closer to Eliza in the way a child might huddle next to their parent for warmth. It wasn't too far of a walk to the street where they both lived and in a few minutes, both women were sitting in front of a small pot-bellied stove, waiting for the heat to flow from the black iron and into the rest of the room.

Eliza lived in a room she'd been renting ever since she'd gotten steady employment at the saloon. There wasn't much space, but there was plenty for her. And that was just the way she liked it.

Setting a small kettle on top of the stove, Eliza removed her coat and wrapped herself in a thick blanket which had been knitted by her grandmother. "I have another blanket if you'd like one."

"Yes, please," Sadie said, looking more like her normal, chipper self.

Already, Eliza was starting to wonder what she'd started by inviting this woman into her home. "It'll take a while for the water to boil. Why don't you tell me more about what happened to put the fright into you?"

The cheeriness faded away from Sadie's face and she stared down at her feet. "He was just some man who was in the Mountainside. He seemed like he was ready to leave with someone and when I saw you walk away . . . I decided to try my own luck."

Eliza's eyes went wide. "*That's* the man you're talking about? Do you know who he is?"

"No. Should I?"

She was about to say more, but Eliza knew she'd only start yelling if she did. Instead, she decided not to scare the other woman and try to find out what had happened. Emotions aside, she was still curious. "So what happened?"

"I . . . did my job and was about to leave when he started looking at me in a strange way. It was like he wanted to hurt me. I don't know how I knew, but I could just feel it. You know what I mean?"

"Yes," Eliza said as her anger melted away. "Every girl who does the job we do knows what you mean. It happens sometimes."

"Well I never felt anything like this. I mean, I've had cowboys get out of hand when they're feeling randy and all, but it wasn't never anything I couldn't handle."

"So what made this one different?"

A chill seemed to run through Sadie's body which had nothing to do with the weather. In fact, the stove was starting to heat up and Eliza had been just about to shed her blanket.

"Those others may have been rough," Sadie confided. "But they were still just mean. This man was . . ." Pausing, she looked up at Eliza as if she was still seeking the older woman's approval. "This man was evil. I could feel it right down to my bones."

Hearing those words sent a chill through Eliza's body to match the one being felt by Sadie. Clutching the blanket tighter around her, she turned toward the stove and kept herself busy by preparing the tea that she'd promised to make. It was nice to occupy herself, but it wasn't nearly enough to make her feel much better.

TWENTY-SEVEN

As tired as Clint was after the day he'd had, the very thought of going to sleep didn't appeal to him in the least. He eventually made his way into the same hotel as Gordon and the rest of his men, but had second thoughts before signing his name to the register.

Trying not to be too noticeable, Clint turned and left the hotel. After hearing all that Cam had said on the way into town, it suddenly seemed like a bad idea to sleep too close to that crew. They might not mind the idea of having a mad-dog killer after them, but Clint sure didn't relish the thought. Besides, he figured that walking about for a while to find a stable and another hotel would tire him out so that he could get some sleep.

Just as he was about to walk away, Clint caught sight of a figure standing in the hotel that was watching him through the narrow rectangular window cut into the door. It was Cam. And when he saw that Clint was leaving, he gave an easy wave and headed for the staircase leading to the rooms.

Allyn's Mill wasn't too big of a place. Clint gathered that much after walking its streets for ten minutes or so. In that time, he'd already gotten in sight of the other end of town. Luckily, there was a stable in sight that had plenty of room for Eclipse. Once the Darley Arabian had a place to sleep, Clint figured it was time to find one for himself.

According to the stable boy, there was only one hotel in town that was worth the price of a room. Besides that, there were some boardinghouses here and there as well as some expensive rooms on the upper floor of the Mountainside Tavern. Since Clint didn't feel like trying to sleep above a saloon, he kept roaming the streets and keeping his eyes peeled for one of those boardinghouses.

In the darkness, the cold seemed especially bitter. But Clint didn't feel it too much since the chill reminded him that he was still alive. With all the talk of death, blood and murder, Clint appreciated the simple knowledge that he was all right and healthy.

At least . . . he was for the moment, anyway.

He didn't run into too many folks during his walk. Clint figured that was due more to the weather than the hour. Despite the fact that it was pitch-black and still as a funeral outside, it was still not even ten o'clock. Most of the signs of life he encountered were coming from within one of the other buildings he passed along the way.

Of the few souls he saw on the street, one of them was a slim figure of a man dressed in a simple jacket which came down to just past his knees. He walked with his arms folded over his chest and hands tucked beneath them, with his head held tilted downward so that the lower part of his face would be covered by the thick wool scarf wrapped around his neck.

Clint barely took any notice of the other man until he was just about to walk past him. At that moment, the man lifted his head and gave him a quick, polite nod.

"Evening, sir," the man said.

Clint returned the nod and added a friendly smile of his own. "Good evening to you."

"Are you new to this good town?"

Stopping after he'd already gone a couple paces past the other man, Clint turned so he could look into his eyes. "Is it that obvious?"

Smiling, the man lowered his eyes as though he was slightly embarrassed. "I don't mean to pry, sir. Just seeing if you might need some directions." The man uncrossed his arms and extended a hand in greeting. When he did, his coat came open just enough to reveal the hint of black beneath his coat. Below his scarf, the bottom edge of a white collar could just be seen.

"Oh," Clint said when he recognized the clothing from what little he'd seen. "I appreciate the help, Father. Is that right?"

"Been a while before you've been inside the house of God?"

"Uh . . . yes, actually. I don't get a lot of time to attend services. And I don't usually stay in one place very long, so I've fallen behind on confession as well."

"No need to explain," the priest said. "I'm Father Planter."

Clint was glad to be off the hook. He had to smile at how he'd suddenly felt like a young boy who was being called out for skipping Sunday School. "Clint Adams. And actually, I could use some advice since I just rode into town."

"The only hotel I'd recommend is actually down the—"

"Thank you, but no," Clint interrupted. "Actually, I'm looking for something closer to a boardinghouse."

"Ahh, I see. You prefer a homier atmosphere."

"You can say that. Also, the food's usually a little better than in a hotel. It would be the closest thing I've had to a home-cooked meal in a while."

"That's a pity, Mister Adams. But you do happen to be in luck. The woman in this house right here accepts boarders," Father Planter said while pointing toward a two-level building a bit farther down the street. "And she's also a fine cook. She used to run a restaurant here in town, from what I gather. It certainly shows."

"Much obliged, Father. I won't keep you in the cold any longer. Thanks again for the help."

"You can repay me by visiting me in my chapel. It's on the northern edge of town. It's small, but you won't miss it. I'd be happy to hear your confession."

Clint was starting to get that tossing in his gut again as he started trying to think of a way to get out of promising anything that would involve getting up early. "Actually, I might not be the best of company in the morning. Rough ride and all."

"Then stop by whenever you feel like it. I'm there most of the day."

Looking into the priest's kind face, it was hard for Clint to refuse. "All right. I'll see you then."

"Splendid. Sleep well, Mister Adams. I think I will be heading home myself."

After even that short of a conversation, Clint could tell that Father Planter did his fair share of damage to the locals' wallets whenever the collection plate came around. Glad to be on his way before promising anything else, Clint opened the door to the boardinghouse and stepped inside.

TWENTY-EIGHT

The woman who let Clint inside was exactly as he'd imagined she would be after listening to Father Planter's brief description. Although the priest hadn't given any physical specifics, Clint had heard enough to form a picture in his mind.

Sure enough, the woman had gray hair piled up on top of her head in a thick bun. She was wrapped in a couple of drab shawls, which only added to her considerable bulk. Even with all the material covering her frame, it was more than obvious that she'd spent a good deal of her life working in the kitchen. She was the shape of a pumpkin and her cheeks looked as though they'd been made from soft dough.

"Come in, come in," she'd said the moment Clint opened the door. "Hurry up before you let all the cold in."

Clint did as he was told and nearly caught a backhand from the old woman when he began to walk into the foyer.

"Wipe your feet on the mat for God's sake," the old woman scolded. "Were you raised in a barn?"

"No, ma'am."

"Then be thorough about it and make sure that you don't dirty up my floors. I just cleaned them this afternoon."

"Yes, ma'am."

Watching as her new arrival scrubbed the bottom of his boots against the rough mat setting just inside the doorway, she didn't step aside until she was satisfied that he'd done a good enough job. Her eyes remained fixed on him, however, and she followed at least three steps behind when Clint walked toward a small desk along a nearby wall.

"I'm here for a room," Clint said. "Is there a book you need me to sign for me to get a key?"

"Who're you after, stranger?"

"Pardon me, ma'am?"

"If it's that poor, frightened girl, you can just forget it. I'll call the sheriff and be done with you rather than let you lay a finger on that scared little thing."

Trying not to let his frustration show too badly, Clint shrugged and held out his hands. "I honestly don't know what you're talking about, ma'am. All I need is a place to sleep and a meal tomorrow morning. If you don't want to accept my money, then I can move on."

The old woman stared at him with light-green, slightly clouded eyes. She was just about to say something when she was stopped by a voice that came from the staircase at the back of the room.

"It's all right, Mrs. Tristip," the voice said. "He's not the one you have to worry about."

The old woman glanced toward the stairs, her features instantly brightening. "Are you sure, sweetie? I would hate to let someone in that might harm one of my favorite boarders."

Eliza came down the stairs and walked straight over to Mrs. Tristip. "I know who Sadie was talking about and this isn't him. So you'd best start treating him a little kinder before you chase away a paying customer."

"Oh dear," Mrs. Tristip said while placing her hands upon her cheeks. "You're right, of course." Turning to Clint, she said, "I am so sorry, young man. We've had a bit of a scare tonight and I was just trying to be careful. Of course there's a room for you and I'll fix you the best breakfast you've ever had."

Startled by the old woman's transformation, Clint decided to play the cards he was dealt before the owner of the boardinghouse switched her mood again. "That sounds wonderful. How much for the room?"

"Don't worry about that right now. I'll get your key and you get upstairs to get some rest. You look like you need it."

Seeing as how he was starting to feel the entire day pressing down on his shoulders, Clint was in no position to argue. He didn't know which would betray him first; the bags under his eyes or the stoop in his spine.

Eliza made her way across the room, walked past Clint and moved to Mrs. Tristip's side. Leaning in close to the old woman's ear, she said softly, "I appreciate your concern for me. Really, I do. But you know how I feel about you listening in to my conversations."

"I would never—"

"The walls are thin," Eliza interrupted. "I know because I've lived here awhile. And Sadie didn't say a word about being afraid until my door was closed."

The old woman sighed heavily and pulled open a drawer in the desk. "It's just that I worry about you, dear," she said while removing one of the keys inside the drawer. "And that other girl looked so frightened."

"She was, but we're fine. Thank you, Mrs. Tristip."

"I'll keep my nose to my own affairs, then." And this time, the old woman said that loud enough for anyone in the room to hear. Judging by the look on her face, someone who didn't know any better might have thought that

Eliza had just smacked Mrs. Tristip on the nose.

Holding out the key for Clint, Mrs. Tristip looked up at him sternly. "Your room is at the top of the stairs, second door on the left. There's ladies here as well so be sure to mind your—"

Eliza cleared her throat loudly.

Hearing that, Mrs. Tristip held up her hands and turned to leave the room. "All right. Fine. Do whatever you want. I'll just collect your money, throw the food on the table and mind my own business." Acting as though she was fully expecting someone to stop her, the old woman rushed out of the room and headed to the kitchen.

Neither Clint nor Eliza lifted a finger to get in her way.

"What was that about?" Clint asked.

Eliza smiled and shrugged. "She's just a little over-protective. She didn't mean to give you that look."

"It sounds like you're pretty familiar with that look yourself."

"More than I care to admit." Smiling, the slender brunette extended her hand. "I'm Eliza Morrow."

"Clint Adams," he replied, accepting her hand inside his own.

She looked him up and down, obviously interested in what she saw. As they smiled at each other, Eliza felt the weariness from the day start to fade and she thought she might have sensed the same thing coming from this new arrival.

Clint wasn't too quick to leave. Not that he minded taking an extra couple of seconds to enjoy the sight of Eliza's trim, alluring figure. On the contrary, he thought he'd be perfectly comfortable watching her for a good, long time. But he'd also picked up on something else that made him hesitant to pick up his things and leave.

"Is there something wrong here?" Clint asked.

Eliza shifted on her feet nervously. "No. Why do you ask?"

"Mrs. Tristip isn't the only one with a keen ear. She seemed really worried about something. And I thought I heard her say that someone was frightened about some—"

"Never mind," she snapped. "It's not your problem."

As much as Clint wanted to find out what was going on, he hadn't been having much luck when it came to appeasing his curiosity lately. And since the brunette didn't seem too forthcoming, Clint decided to let things lie right where they'd fallen and stay out of it for a change. "You're right," he said. "It's just a shame to see such a pretty face so upset. If you'd like someone to talk to, you know where I'll be."

The cautious part of Eliza's brain wanted to be upset with Clint. But when he smiled and turned to walk away, she wanted nothing more than to take him up on his offer right then and there. But there was something that kept her from acting on that impulse. Or rather, there was some*one* who kept her from going any further.

Sadie was still upstairs and waiting for Eliza to return with more firewood. Storing away the location of Clint's room in the back of her mind, Eliza hurried to get the firewood and rushed upstairs.

TWENTY-NINE

For someone who enjoyed the darkness, the coldest months of the year were also some of the most comfortable. More than simply enjoying the long nights, Jessup also had a coldness that ran throughout his entire body, permeating his heart and flowing through his blood. For a man like him, this winter was like heaven.

He stood outside, leaning up against the side of a building while trying to look like he was just as cold as the few people who walked by. For the most part, those others were too concerned with getting where they were going and didn't seem to pay Jessup any mind. But just to be sure, the killer shoved his hands deep into his pockets and put on a tense, trembling face so that he looked just as weak as everyone else.

Staring up at the upper windows of the boardinghouse, Jessup waited for the woman to walk by her shade one more time. The light in her room was faint, but just enough to make her shadow appear for him whenever she got up to walk around. He didn't have to wait long before the familiar figure stood up, stretched her back and bent over to tend to something he couldn't see. He'd been watching the shadow play for a while now. What kept his interest was the fact that he knew exactly who was up there and exactly what she was talking about.

Even though he could only see the shadow going through the motions of speaking, he didn't have to hear her words to know precisely what they were. She was scared. She was frightened. She was worried that something might happed to cause her pain.

She was scared of him.

Now, that thought managed to put a smile on Jessup's face. Thinking back to the feel of him on her lap, the sensation of her naked skin on his, the sight of her on his bed, the feel of him fucking her . . . all of that washed through Jessup's mind in a rush, making the cold feel that much warmer.

He was concerned that she might have gone to someone and talk about what scared her. At the time she'd left his room, Sadie had seemed a little skittish, but mostly aloof. She was a professional girl, which was why he'd picked her. But Jessup sensed the trace of fear that ran just beneath her surface and had followed her here to see how she might act on that.

A part of him was hoping that she would simply go home and forget about her night's work. That would have made everything so much simpler. But, Jessup knew that if she really wasn't worried about anything, she would have gone back to the Mountainside so she could pick up another willing customer.

Then again, no matter how much simpler that would have been, it sure wouldn't have been any fun.

Jessup had actually felt glad when he saw the way Sadie talked to Eliza. When he saw that she was worried and wanting to share those worries with someone else, Jessup felt a subtle twinge of joy in the pit of his stomach.

Now he had a reason to kill her. And the other one . . . the brunette. Now, he could kill her, too.

Such pleasant thoughts filled Jessup's mind, but he

didn't allow them to occupy him completely. As much as he would have liked to wait a bit longer before slipping into the boardinghouse so he could take care of his business, the killer knew that would not be such a good idea. The arrival of Clint Adams had blown that whole plan to hell.

Jessup recognized Adams when he'd ambushed Gordon's men outside of town. Traveling in his circles, Jessup would have recognized Adams by reputation alone. But when he'd been sighting in on those men, Jessup managed to spot Adams creeping in toward the clearing.

Adams moved like some kind of predatory cat. He was smooth, calm and sure of himself. Even before he found out who Adams was, Jessup would have considered him a threat. But now, the newest arrival was more than just a threat.

He was a famous threat.

And when Jessup finally managed to take down Adams as well as Gordon and all of his men, the killer would become a legend.

No matter how much Jessup enjoyed his chosen profession, it would feel so good to get the kind of recognition that Adams's death would bring. And the more he thought about it, the more anxious Jessup became to get started. When he looked at the boardinghouse, he saw so much more than door, walls and windows. He saw blind spots, places to hide, places to enter and places to escape. He saw through the eyes of a sniper, which tore everything down to its barest of essentials.

It was a skill he'd acquired over time and through plenty of practice.

But that would have to wait. Adams had been around for a long time and it was common knowledge among those who knew anything about him that the Gunsmith didn't let go of a problem once he'd sunken his teeth into it.

Gordon, on the other hand, was tired. Even Cam Winslow was tired. And if those two were tired, that meant every one of their men had to be ready to fall over. Jessup was sure that most of them were probably asleep already, confident that they knew how he thought and what he was going to do next. Well, Jessup was anxious to see the look on their faces when they realized that they'd been wrong.

Dead wrong.

His eyes still fixed on those upper windows, Jessup watched for another minute or two until a new light flickered to life behind a window that had been dark since he'd arrived. Jessup shifted his focus to that window and smiled grimly. That had to be Adams's room. In fact, Jessup was sure of it since he hadn't seen anyone else go into that boardinghouse except for Adams and the two women.

Nodding silently, Jessup waited for another lone figure to walk by before he lifted his hands as though he was holding an invisible rifle. Like a child playing war, he twitched his finger upon the imaginary trigger just like he would when the Gunsmith's time finally came.

But Clint Adams wasn't next to die. There was someone else who had that distinct privilege and he was waiting for his bullet in the hotel a few blocks away.

Jessup placed his hands into his pockets, lowered his head, and instantly became just another one of the figures making their way through a cold, dark night.

THIRTY

Clint's room was small.

He'd rented plenty of rooms in plenty of towns in his day, and every one of them had their own distinct flavor. When he'd unlocked his door and turned the knob of the lantern sitting on a table just inside this particular room, only one word came to mind.

Small.

And taking another closer look at the place didn't do a bit to help him add to that opinion.

It was just big enough to hold a small bed, a small dresser and just enough floor space for him to walk around between them. The bed was just the right size for an average sized man . . . alone. Even if Clint was spending the night with the most beautiful, sensuous woman he could imagine, there still wouldn't be enough room for both of them to get any sleep in that bed. On the other hand, it looked plenty soft and was covered with several thick blankets and, despite its size, looked rather inviting at the moment.

Clint dropped his gear in one corner and took a seat on the edge of the bed. It squeaked slightly beneath his weight, but felt awful good after spending most of his day in the saddle. The dresser was the only other thing in the room. Its drawers were empty and there was a pair of pictures in frames on top. Clint could only guess that the people in the photographs were Mrs. Tristip's family and, like most other people in such pictures, they looked straight-faced and severe.

After allowing himself to relax for a moment, Clint felt that familiar uneasy tingle coming from the bottom of his stomach. He hadn't allowed himself to put the thought of Jessup aside as well as the others. And besides the general weariness of knowing there was a heartless killer about, he still wanted to find some other way to verify Cam's story.

The best way he could think of to do that was to see if anyone else had heard about the murders he'd described. Clint's first impression was that he might have a hard time finding someone to fit that bill in this particular town. But, he knew first-hand that news traveled quickly. And morbid news traveled that much quicker.

But that wasn't what set Clint's nerves on end. That had come from the fact that he'd started to relax the moment his body touched down on the comfortable bed. And if that had happened to him, then he figured Cam's men would fade away even faster. And if he was a sniper looking to pick one of those men off, now would be the time he would have chosen.

As much as he hated to do it, Clint pulled himself up off the bed and back onto his feet. Now that he'd sampled it, the mattress seemed to call his name. The room suddenly didn't seem small, but soothing. There were little touches left behind by Mrs. Tristip that appealed to Clint the more he looked at them. And the longer he stood there, the rattling of the windows being shaken from the wind seemed to get louder and louder.

"Aww, hell," Clint groaned to himself as he pulled on his coat and slapped his hat back onto his head.

There would be plenty of time for him to rest once he'd put his mind at ease. And if his concerns turned out to be nothing, then he could get back to this small, comfortable room and crawl under those thick blankets. But if his instincts were correct, then he might be needed pretty soon, if only to make sure that nobody else got hurt if all of Cam's men decided to open fire.

Unfortunately, Clint had learned the hard way that his instincts were rarely wrong.

Once he'd managed to get out of the room and turn the key in the lock, Clint took a deep breath and set himself to his task. He strode down the hall and was at the top of the steps in a few paces. As he started to descend, he heard a door open directly behind him.

"Mister Adams?" came a familiar voice.

Clint stopped and turned to look over his shoulder, even though he already knew who it was. "What is it, Eliza?"

If she was taken aback by his brusque manner, Eliza didn't show it. "Actually, I was just walking out my . . . friend here when I heard your door open. You seemed to be in a hurry, so I thought it best if I stay out of your way."

Just then, Clint could see another woman coming out of Eliza's room. Although this one looked somewhat younger and had longer hair, she didn't have Eliza's natural charm. Just from that one glimpse, Clint could tell which of the two women he would rather spend any time with. When Clint spotted the redness in the younger girl's eyes, he remembered what Mrs. Tristip said about someone being frightened by something or other.

"If you'd like some company," Clint said in a softer tone, "I'd be more than happy to see you both to where you need to go."

Although the younger girl looked happy at that prospect, Eliza shook her head in refusal. "There won't be a need for that," she said. "Sadie just lives right across the street and I think I can handle it on my own."

Clint saw disappointment reflected in Sadie's eyes. But more important, he didn't feel comfortable leaving both women on their own when he, himself, was out looking for a madman. "I was heading out myself and if it's just across the street, it won't be out of my way at all."

"Thank you, Clint, but—"

"No," he interrupted while raising a finger in the air. "I insist."

From where he was, all Clint had to do if he wanted to touch Eliza's skin was to extend his arm just a few more inches. He knew he wanted to do just that, but he wasn't too sure about whether or not the gesture would be appreciated. Her face looked so soft and her skin was so creamy that Clint's imagination started running away with what it would be like to feel it for himself. He could almost feel his hands moving over her body, slowly at first, and then building to a more passionate frenzy.

By the look on Eliza's face, she was thinking about something along those same lines, if only for a brief moment. But then she rolled her eyes and let out a frustrated breath as Sadie bumped past her to head down the stairs.

"I don't care what Eliza says," Sadie chirped. "I'd appreciate an escort very much." Taking hold of Clint's elbow, she added, "Very, very much."

"Looks like you're outvoted," Clint said.

Eliza followed them down the stairs and hooked her arm through Clint's other elbow. "If I'm outvoted, then I might as well enjoy myself."

Clint led them both outside and left Sadie at the door to where she rented her own room. All the while, Clint's eyes were roaming the streets and shadows, watching for any movement that didn't seem right or any sound that seemed out of place. He was waiting for a shot to break the silence and slice through the air.

He didn't know why, since Gordon and the rest of his

men were down the street, but Clint thought that one of the women knew something that might put their lives in danger.

But that shot never came. All he saw were plain old shadows and the occasional passer-by who kept their heads down and their noses in their own affairs.

Once Sadie was safely inside her building, Clint turned back toward the street with one woman still on his arm. "I guess this is where we should part ways," he said. "I've got some matters to tend to and I'd hate to keep you out in the cold."

"Oh," Eliza said, unable to hide all of her disappointment. "Well then, I'll let you go." She hung on to his arm for another couple of seconds before reluctantly breaking away from Clint's side. "When you get back, knock on my door. Maybe we can talk."

"I'd like that . . . if it's not too late."

"Me too."

After watching Eliza step back inside the boarding-house, Clint turned on the balls of his feet and strode toward the hotel. He was still waiting for that bullet to come from the darkness and something in his gut told him that he wouldn't have to wait much longer.

THIRTY-ONE

Clint had just walked past the Mountainside Tavern when he saw the pair of dark figures standing outside the hotel where Cam and the rest were staying. Slowing his pace down to something that wouldn't make him so noticeable, Clint took his hands out of his coat pockets and let them fall loosely at his sides. That way, he would be ready to draw if everything went to hell.

Lowering his eyes while keeping as much to the shadows as possible, he continued down the street. Clint knew that he'd already been spotted by the pair of men standing outside the hotel. Although he still couldn't make out their eyes from where he was standing, he could tell by the way they shifted to face him that those two were studying him just as hard as he was studying them.

The instant his hand got anywhere near his gun belt, Clint could sense the two figures become tense. One of them was carrying a shotgun and he hefted that up into both hands, preparing himself to fire.

Clint might not have been able to see details of their faces, but he was certainly able to hear the sound of both of those hammers being snapped back on the shotgun. He stopped where he was and held his hands out slightly to either side.

"Don't waste a shot on me," Clint said. "Especially when you've got a better target wandering around somewhere."

"What the hell are you doin' out here, Adams?" one of the figures said. The voice alone was enough to reveal his identity, but just to be sure, Gordon stepped closer so that Clint could see him.

Clint tipped his hat. "Good evening to you. I couldn't get any sleep."

"So you just thought you'd wander out here in this cold, huh?" Gordon asked. "It's a helluva lot warmer inside the hotel, but you wouldn't know about that. What's the matter, Adams? Too nervous about bein' close the next time Jessup shows his face?"

"Actually . . . yes. And maybe you should be too."

Gordon walked up so that he was about five feet in front of where Clint was standing. "Aw, shit. I guess I can't blame you none. What're you doin' out here?"

"Something told me that Jessup might just show his face around this part of town. Especially after running you and your men ragged earlier in the day."

"Yeah. I thought that myself . . . for about the first month or two. But when Jessup still kept himself scarce, I figured he just liked watching us act scared."

"So you don't think he'll be here?"

"Nah. Probably not."

"Is that why you and your partner here posted yourself as guards in the middle of the night?" Clint asked. "Or is that just your way of acting scared?"

"Better safe than sorry, you might say. Besides, what concern is it of yours what happens to us? By the way you snuck out on us, I thought you were set to go your own way."

"Oh, believe me, I am definitely set to go my own way.

But I've got this nasty habit of lending my hand where it's needed."

"And you think it's needed here?" Gordon asked.

"Yes, I do."

"Even after we've been the one hunting this animal all this time?"

"Have you caught him yet?"

"No," Gordon replied warily.

"Then . . . yes. I'd say you most definitely needed some fresh help."

For a moment, Gordon looked as though he hadn't taken kindly to Clint's words. Actually, for a brief second, he seemed about one step away from taking a swing at the man in front of him. But before he did anything so drastic, his face broke into an ugly smile and he shook his head.

"Have you been listening to this bullshit, Underhill?" Gordon bellowed.

"Yes, I have," the man behind Gordon replied.

Clint glanced over Gordon's shoulder and saw that the figure who'd been holding the shotgun was the same man who'd tried unsuccessfully to ride Eclipse. "I hear that Cam was actually about to shoot my horse before you stepped in," Clint said.

"Really?"

"Yeah. Cam mentioned it on the way into town. That was a great thing you did. It might have not been too smart to try and ride him yourself, but I still thank you all the same."

"No problem," Underhill said.

Clint stepped forward and shook the other man's hand. That simple gesture alone seemed to soften the tension between him and the other two men. The group of men were like a close-knit troop of soldiers and Clint was the outsider. It would take a lot more for them to stop looking at him with suspicion, but this was at least a step in the right direction.

Underhill shook Clint's hand vigorously. "No problem at all. Actually, I was thinking of keeping that fine horse of yours for mysel—"

There was a sharp *crack*, which echoed from one of the buildings across the street and a single bullet hissed through the air. The next sound was that of lead slapping against flesh and before Clint could so much as blink, he felt a warm mist spray onto his face.

Underhill was still looking straight at him, his face frozen in the same casual expression that he'd worn when talking about Eclipse. But the life in his eyes was quickly fading away. It reminded Clint of the way a candle wick still glowed for a bit after the flame had been snuffed. The next thing Clint noticed was the fresh hole in Underhill's skull just below the brim of his hat.

Still gripping Underhill's hand, Clint saw the other man slump backward and fall to the ground. A split-second before the body hit, Clint's reflexes snapped into full speed and he twisted around to get a look at what was going on.

Gordon was in mid-draw and was just about to clear leather.

Across the street, in a darkened building, there was one window opened halfway to allow the end of a rifle barrel to peek out into the night. Before Clint could act, the rifle barked again.

THIRTY-TWO

When it came to instincts, Clint knew that there was a certain way to treat the impulses that coursed through his body just as they did in any other animal's. There were times to hold them back and times to let them flow freely. And then there were also times to let those instincts pitch the rest of him straight down to the ground, even if it meant eating a mouthful of dirty snow.

Before Clint even had a chance to think about what he should do or what he was doing, he was dropping straight down and pressing his face against the cold, gritty ground. It was those same instincts that ordered him to roll toward the building where he could at least use the raised boardwalk for some degree of cover.

He didn't know where that second shot had landed, but he did know that it hadn't landed inside him. And for the moment, that was the most important thing. Once he was certain that he could still move and wasn't hurt, Clint set about seeing what he could do for the others.

It may have seemed selfish in hindsight, but that was instincts for you. They were never much for courtesy.

"Gordon, are you hit?" Clint asked as both shots still echoed through his ears.

The other man was on the ground right beside Clint. His breath curling out from between clenched teeth like steam from a bull's mouth, Gordon was searching the darkness with quick, darting eyes. "I ain't hit. That son of a bitch is savin' me for last. Hell, I could probably walk on out of here without getting a scratch on me."

Another shot cracked through the night, followed by the hiss of incoming lead. There was a spark and a dull thump as the bullet drilled into the wall less than six inches over Gordon's head.

"Then again," he said. "I could be wrong."

Clint's hand was on the handle of his Colt and he drew up his legs beneath him so that he would be ready to move. "Something tells me Jessup's changed his own rules. But there's one thing he can't change, and that's the fact that we know where he is."

"Yer damn right about that," Gordon said while bringing his pistol up and thumbing back the hammer. "My boys'll be right behind me any time, but I ain't about to wait for 'em."

"I was hoping you'd say that."

And without letting another moment slip by, Clint and Gordon sprung up from their position, immediately charging toward the building across the street. Not sure of whether he would have to dodge or shoot first, Clint kept the Colt in its holster. That way, there was no way for it to slip out of his hand if he had to jump for cover and he always knew that he could draw it in less than a moment's notice if the need arose.

For the moment, Clint was too concerned about the next rifle shot, which could have come at any second as he and Gordon crossed the street. Even though it took all of two or three seconds, that trip from one side of the street to the other seemed as though it was never going to end. As he ran, Clint thought about all he'd heard about Jessup. That, coupled with the demonstration he'd had for himself, made him fully confident that the killer could pick him off at any time if he so desired.

Luckily, that mood didn't seem to hit since both men made it to the front of the darkened building alive and unharmed.

He and Gordon pressed their backs against the wall on either side of the door. "Check this door and I'll go around back," Clint said. "Just be sure to look for me before you start shooting once we're both inside."

Gordon acknowledged Clint with a quick nod and tried the door handle. It was locked, but Gordon stepped in front of it and prepared to kick it down as Clint moved around the side wall on his way to the back of the building.

The sound of Gordon's boot smashing against wood followed Clint as he rounded the rear corner and hopped up onto a small back porch. As he'd figured, the back door was open. Clint thought that, although Jessup might be in too big of a hurry to mess around with climbing through windows, he wasn't dumb enough to simply walk in through the front door. And if anyone was going to get ahold of this killer that night, Clint figured it might as well be him.

Pushing open the door, Clint kept his head down and his hand upon his modified Colt while rushing into the building. Since he couldn't see through to the front room, Clint could only hear Gordon's heavy footsteps as the other man charged inside. Judging by the shape of the room, there was a staircase near the entrance. Clint kept his steps as light as possible as he made his way toward the dark, rectangular outline which he hoped was a door.

The inside of the room was almost completely dark. There were no lanterns lit and not even a candle to guide his way. But the night was clear enough and the moon bright enough to shine some bit of illumination through the windows, if only to let Clint move without running smack into a wall or doorjamb.

Now that he was inside, Gordon seemed to be taking some care to keep quiet, but his efforts weren't enough to let anyone in the dark know exactly where he was. Clint hoped the other man was at least a good shot. Otherwise, he might not make it out in time to see the next sunrise.

Clint kept his left hand extended so he could feel along the wall as he kept moving forward. When he came to the door, he pushed it open and it swung easily upon greased hinges. But rather than see the vague outlines of the next room, all Clint could see was blackness. He felt suddenly tense, as if he was just about to walk into a brick wall.

But that was no wall in front of him. It was the outline of a man that was standing directly in front of him.

For a brief moment, Clint thought that he'd almost run into Gordon. But then he heard the sound of Gordon's footsteps working their way up the stairs in the next room. The next thing he heard was a light, raspy voice, which sounded colder than the wind outside.

"Hey Adams," it whispered. "Guess who's next to die?"

THIRTY-THREE

Still unable to focus on anything but the dark, shadowy outline of the man in front of him, Clint's mind raced with all the important things he needed to know to survive the next minute or two. First among them was the fact that, whoever this was, he couldn't see Clint any better in the dark than Clint could see him.

As for Clint's body . . . it was already snapping into motion.

Fueled by his finely honed reflexes, Clint's hand tightened around his Colt and drew it from its holster. As he did that, his legs were carrying him to the side while twisting his upper body so that he was still facing the dark figure.

Clint's back slammed against something solid, which moved back a couple inches amid a jarring clatter. As soon as dull pain from the impact started to pulse through his body, the room was lit up with the brief flash of gunfire.

Within the confined space, the shot was almost deafening. But even so, Clint knew that the gun hadn't been the same one that had been fired at them when he and Gordon were still outside. The blast was more explosive, meaning that it probably came from a high-caliber pistol rather than a rifle.

Even so, that didn't mean that Clint wasn't instantly thankful that he wasn't standing in front of it when it had gone off.

That quick flash caused his vision to be filled with dull, glowing red blobs. Clint fought to see through them, but knew he wasn't going to be able to do that for another couple of seconds. Rather than wait for that to happen, he swung out with his left fist.

All he caught was a glancing blow. The sound of scuffling feet could be heard through the ringing in his ears.

"I expected better from you, Adams," came the rough voice once again.

"And you'll get it," Clint replied.

With that last blow, Clint hadn't been trying to do any damage. Instead, his intention had been to get a feel of where the other man was in the darkness. What he'd felt of the man's jaw gave him a piece of that, while the sound of footsteps painted an even better picture in Clint's mind. Using that knowledge, Clint held his Colt low, aimed and squeezed the trigger.

The blast from Clint's Colt was almost as deafening as the last shot. But since he was behind the muzzle rather than in front of it, he got a better look at his target in the split-second of light the shot had provided.

Clint had been ready for that muzzle flash and had prepared his eyes to soak up as much as possible. What he saw was a man that was roughly his own size, wearing dark clothes and holding a pistol in one hand. The other hand had been thrown up reflexively in front of his face and his head was turning away. The spray of blood coming from the other man's left shoulder looked like a grainy photograph frozen by the strobe of light.

As the roar of gunfire died down again, Clint was on the move since that last shot had marked his own position just as well as it had marked his attacker. Crouching down low and sidestepping to his right, Clint moved in an almost serpentine fashion from one set of shadows into another.

Judging by the sound of footsteps, the other man had the same idea and was quickly trying to find another angle from which to strike.

Once both men had abandoned their previous spots, the noise in the room faded quickly away. There was only the soft sound of bodies brushing against unseen objects and the light undercurrent of their suppressed breathing.

Clint's eyes were adjusting to the darkness somewhat, but not enough to make him sure exactly where the attacker was. He knew that the other man was practically right in front of him, but if Clint made one wrong move and missed his opportunity, he would do nothing but advertise exactly where he was so that the other man could finish him off.

Suddenly, there was a loud thumping sound. In the tense silence, it resembled a wild bull rampaging down a hallway. But it was only Gordon thundering down the stairs. Compared to the silence that both men had been trying to keep in the dark, Gordon's footsteps were like hammers pounding against every wall inside the building.

"Adams? Where are ya?"

Clint gritted his teeth, hoping that the other man would just shut his mouth and find someplace safe to hide. But then he saw a twitch of motion coming from the shadows. It wasn't much, but it was enough to let him know that there was something moving there that was about his size and carrying something made from dull metal.

That was when Clint realized that Gordon actually was providing a great service. The more noise he made, the more the hidden attacker started to look toward it, which was all Clint needed to pick the other man out from within the darkness.

Since he couldn't even see well enough to sight his gun, Clint focused his eyes on what little he could make out of his target and pointed the Colt as though he was simply pointing his finger at the shadow. Since he'd modified the pistol to be double-action, all he had to do was pull the trigger.

Once again, the Colt roared through the room, illuminating it briefly as it sent a bullet into the air. Even though he could only see the other man for a split-second, he could tell that he was already trying to move away. He couldn't be sure, but Clint thought he might have heard a pained grunt beneath the echo of gunfire.

Without hesitation, Clint surged forward into the dark. He led with his shoulder while keeping the pistol gripped tightly at his side. Hearing the other man cocking back the hammer of his pistol, Clint kept right on moving, hoping that he could make contact before his opponent had a chance to pull the trigger.

Clint's shoulder slammed into something solid. It had to be the other man since it didn't feel like wood and it gave way the moment he touched it. He could hear an almost feral snarl as the body in front of him swiveled and rolled with the impact of Clint's tackle.

Suddenly, Clint felt a sharp pain in his lower abdomen which he thought might have been caused by bumping into the corner of a table or shelf. But the pain was soon followed by an even sharper agony and the flow of warm wetness which soaked into his shirt.

He'd been stabbed.

THIRTY-FOUR

Clint didn't have to see anything to recognize the distinct pain of a knife wound or the touch of his own blood as it flowed freely from the fresh wound. Even though he knew he couldn't let the wound go too long before he tended to it, Clint wasn't about to let the man who did this simply take his shot and get away.

Still close enough to feel the other man when he swung out with his free hand, Clint got his bearings and used his pain as a fuel to drive him onward. It pumped through his body along with a fresh jolt of adrenaline, causing his legs to carry him forward and his arms to swing out powerfully.

This time, he was trying to inflict some pain of his own. And now that he knew roughly where to strike, it took Clint only two tries before his right hand pounded flush against something solid. The grunt that followed let Clint know he'd landed something better than a glancing blow this time around.

"I got you now, you son of a bitch."

Those words drifted through the air and nearly caused Clint to jump back with surprise since they came from less than a foot or two to his right. He might have taken a swing in that direction if he hadn't recognized the voice as Gordon's.

Clint felt more than saw or heard the motion of something cutting through the air next to his head. It came from the same direction as Gordon's voice and was soon followed by a dull *thump* and another grunt from the third man.

Leaning in for a second shot, Clint heard another movement in the darkness, but this one was more of a rushing hiss. Clint reflexively threw himself down and back, recognizing that sound as a blade slicing through the air with a whole lot of force being thrown behind it.

Clint landed on his left side. As soon as he felt the floor beneath his shoulders, he braced himself and lifted up with his right leg, hoping that he wasn't about to make one hell of a bad move.

But Clint's instincts had been right. The knife wasn't meant for him, but for Gordon. And just as the attacker leaned in toward the apex of his swing, Clint's leg caught his forearm to stop the blade before it had been buried into its intended victim.

The instant Clint felt that he'd stopped the swing, he dropped his leg down toward the floor. He wasn't quite fast enough, however, to complete the move before he felt another taste of the blade cutting into his flesh. This time, it wasn't a fast slice, but a strong pull as the blade was set against the back of his shin and its wielder leaned back to dig it in as far as he could.

Feeling the pressure and knowing what was causing it, Clint gritted his teeth and prepared himself for the blazing agony that was about to hit him in full force any second. But rather than wait and take the wound easily, he twisted himself around and swung out with his right hand. He landed the blow a little sooner than he'd been expecting, but wasn't at all disappointed with the result.

Clint heard a wet crunching sound as he slammed the

butt of his pistol into the attacker who was still right in
front of him, but obscured by the shadows. The knife at
his ankle pulled back and there was a solid thump as the
other man fell back onto the floor. Clint was about to get
up when a gunshot went off just behind him and to the
right.

Sparks flew through the air, singing the side of Clint's
head as they sprayed out from Gordon's pistol. The shot
exploded loudly throughout the room, its light displaying
the scene in front of him like a picture that had been taken
in the middle of the night. That image stuck in Clint's
mind as everything else faded back into the familiar darkness.

The attacker had been on the ground and was in the
process of climbing to his feet. With that same image in
his brain, Clint could hear hurried footsteps as the attacker
rushed from the room and toward the back door.

"Oh no you don't," Gordon snarled.

Clint couldn't see Gordon, but he could hear his footsteps charging off in pursuit of the man who'd just fled
the room. Since there was already someone heading for
the back door, Clint decided to take advantage of the fact
that they still outnumbered their attacker and turned to
move toward the front of the building. There was a faint
trickle of silvery light coming from the edges of the front
door, but to Clint, that might as well have been a beacon
blazing in full glory.

He fully expected to have trouble walking on the leg
that had been cut, but when Clint got onto both feet and
started moving, he was glad to feel only a subtle hint of
pain. Knowing that he would have plenty of time to feel
the pain later, he kept working his way through the darkness toward the outline of the front door.

There wasn't much in the room setting between himself
and the door. When Clint got to it, he turned the handle
and opened it. Almost immediately, he was hit by the

contrast between the inside and outside of the building. Even though it was still the middle of the night, the light outside was still stronger than the shadows he'd gotten used to and it took a second or two for him to adjust.

He didn't stop moving, though. Using what he remembered of the outside of the building from when he'd arrived, Clint stepped onto the front porch and started running toward the sound of footsteps rushing around from the back. As far as he could tell, Gordon had flushed out the other man and was chasing him toward the street. Clint placed one hand upon a narrow rail of the steps leading to the boardwalk and hoisted himself up and over. He landed with both feet on the ground. It was at that point he felt the pain from the cut along his ankle.

It was also at that point that Clint heard something else that caught his attention besides the footsteps that were rushing closer toward him.

There must have been at least half a dozen guns being cocked at once. The metallic clatter filled the air and caused Clint to freeze in his tracks like a rabbit that had accidentally run into a field full of hunters.

The footsteps were still coming.

Unfortunately, Clint figured there was also a hail of bullets on its way as well.

THIRTY-FIVE

Every instinct in Clint's head told him to stay perfectly still.

Those were the same instincts that spoke to every animal when they found themselves in someone else's sights, however, and didn't do him a whole lot of good. Even so, it wasn't easy for Clint to fight them back and it was only with the greatest effort that he finally got his head to turn and look toward the source of the sound.

The gunmen were lined up in an uneven row. Some were on both feet and some were down on one knee. Some had rifles. Some had shotguns. Some had pistols. But every one of them were aiming at Clint and they were all one heartbeat away from pulling their triggers.

"Wait," came a voice shouted from the alley between the darkened building and the next. "Don't kill him yet!"

Gordon came rushing toward the boardwalk with his gun held out in front of him. His breaths came in ragged bursts and when he skidded to a stop, he snapped back the hammer of his own pistol. His eyes were full of fire and his lips were curled back in an angry sneer. When he saw who it was at the end of his barrel, however, that expression turned into one of distinct surprise and con-fusion.

"Adams?" Gordon said. "What the hell . . . ?" Noticing that all of his men were about to fire, Gordon looked at them and commanded them to lower their weapons. "Track down the other man that I chased out of that alley. And be quick about it. I don't want him to get away."

One of the men in the line stepped forward. It was the young Indian who all the others called Rico. "Other man? What other man?"

"Don't even talk like that," Gordon snarled. "I was on his tail coming out of that there building and the last time I saw him he was just rounding the corner. I even heard his boots hitting the boardwalk right before I . . ." His words trailed off as his eyes found Clint once again. Gordon's jaw clenched when he realized that Clint himself had probably been the one stomping over the boardwalk. ". . . No," he whispered.

Now that the rest of the gunmen had moved their aim away from him, Clint had straightened up and was search-ing the surrounding area for any trace of the man who'd been chased out of the building. All of the others were doing the same thing and not a one of them seemed to pick up on anything that gave them a clue as to what direction they should search first.

"It hasn't been that long," Clint said quickly. "Everyone split up from here and one of us will have to find some-thing."

The men paused for a second until they heard Gordon's voice. "Well you heard the man," he said. "Get goin'!"

With that, they were off and running. Not one of the men had had time to pull on more than their boots and coats before answering Gordon's call. As they scattered in separate directions, their coats flapped open to reveal long underwear and thin cotton shirts. By the looks of it, Clint had been right in guessing that the men would hit their beds the second they'd checked into the hotel.

Clint waited until the men had taken off before starting to move on his own. Rather than simply pick a direction that had been overlooked, he waited until the sound of rushing footsteps began to fade and stepped up onto the stairs leading to the building's front door. He saw Gordon looking at him with a quizzical expression and before the other man could say anything, Clint silenced him by pressing a finger to his lips.

Silence started to fall back onto the street like a sheet being dropped onto a mattress. And just as Clint was about to shift his position, he heard something moving beneath the boards of the small front porch. To his ears, the sound was like blaring trumpets, even though it was actually no louder than something being lightly dragged over snow-covered gravel.

Gordon heard that as well. His eyes narrowed and he choked back the words that he'd been just about to say. Looking back to Clint, he decided to follow the other man's lead as Clint used his fingers to count down from three.

When Clint's last finger was curled back, both men dropped down to the ground. All Gordon had to do was throw himself forward and brace himself with both hands. Since he was standing on the steps, Clint launched himself up and out so that he landed flat on both boots, allowing himself to drop down to both knees.

The sound of slow movement had quickened for a moment before stopping altogether.

Beneath the porch, there was a space that was no more than two feet high, which stretched partly beneath the building itself. Bending down so that he could look into that space, Clint found himself staring at a man who'd managed to crawl into this space and work himself almost to the stairs before being discovered.

Clint was looking straight at this man, but still couldn't

make out much of his face. This time, his view was impeded not by darkness, but by something the other man was holding in front of him as he'd crawled like a worm through the cramped space.

Clint's ears filled with the sound of his own blood rushing through his body. His heart thumped once and seemed to seize in his chest the instant he realized that he was staring right down the barrel of the other man's gun.

His muscles worked on their own to pull him away from that space. When the gun went off, it filled the air with a muffled roar as lead, smoke and sparks were spat out into the air.

Clint staggered back and clutched at his face. The skin beneath his hands was burning and sensitive to the touch. It felt as though hot needles had been sunken beneath his flesh and his mind spun like a whirlwind inside his skull.

There were more shots, but these came from Gordon as he rushed to Clint's side. Round after round punched through the boards until finally the other man was emptying his pistol into the space near Clint's feet.

Although he heard all of this, Clint was hesitant to lend a hand. In fact, he wasn't sure if he could fight any more at all because he'd just realized one thing.

"Dammit," Clint whispered. "I can't see."

THIRTY-SIX

It was Cam who came to Clint's side when the others had disappeared. Still unable to see anything more than a swirling black mass and the occasional gray, Clint stepped over toward the building and stopped at the first solid thing his hand came across. It was the post beside the stairs and he'd managed to move an entire foot and a half.

Cam stepped in front of Clint and was about to wave a hand in front of his eyes when he was stopped by a flicker of motion coming from the bottom of his field of vision. Looking down, he noticed that Clint had drawn his pistol and was aiming it at his gut.

"I may not be able to see right now," Clint said. "But my hearing's just fine."

"It's only me," Cam said, paying Clint the respect of not introducing himself by name. "You can holster that weapon. Everyone's gone."

"Are you sure?"

Cam nodded. Then, realizing what he'd done, said, "Yeah. I'm sure. Once you spotted Jessup under the porch, Gordon took some of the others and chased him off."

"Are you sure it was Jessup? I never did get a good

look at his face." Clint stopped to think a moment. "Then again . . . I've never really gotten a good look at his face."

"It was Jessup all right. I got a look at Underhill's body and he was hit in the same spot as most of the others. And from what I gathered, it sounded like his style of fighting."

Clint put his hand on the post, took it back and made a fist. Venting his frustration, he slammed his fist against the post hard enough to send a shock wave up to the awning and down into the stairs. "This was just great. I wanted to help and not only does one of your men get killed anyway, but Jessup gets away and I get blinded in the process. It might have been him, but there's no way to really tell for sure. I don't care what you said."

"You want better proof?" Cam asked. "Here's your proof." Reaching down, he slapped his hand against the back of Clint's boot, causing him to flinch with sharp pain. "Here's some more proof," Cam added, this time patting his hand against the cut along the bottom row of Clint's ribs. "I'm awful familiar with wounds like those. They were made by a straight razor. The cut on your ribs is thin, but clean and deep. And the one on your leg should've been stopped by your boot, but the blade still got partly through. Only a razor could slice through that much leather."

Clint thumped the post one more time with the side of his hand. It wasn't half as hard as the first blow, but was enough to let out a bit more of the steam that had been building up inside of him. "All right. That was the same guy." Turning toward the area where Cam's voice had been coming from, he said, "I'm sorry about Underhill. He was a good man."

"Better than you know."

The swirling blacks were giving way to more grays. After a couple more seconds, Clint started to notice a difference in the way his eyes were working. Instead of blurred nothingness, he could start to make out shapes mixed in among sparkling red starbursts. "I can almost make out your face. I guess that muzzle flash didn't do as much damage as I'd thought."

"You're damn lucky, Adams. You almost caught a bullet through the skull rather than a face full of sparks."

"That's not saying much. Jessup still got away."

Cam walked over to Clint's side and chucked him on the shoulder. Clint's vision was clearing up enough for him to see the bigger man coming this time.

"We all appreciate what you did," Cam said. "Hell, you didn't even have to come back down here at all. What changed your mind, anyway?"

Rubbing his eyes, Clint pressed his other hand upon the cut in his side. "You fellas seemed a bit too relaxed. I just thought that if anyone was about to take all of you on, he'd have to keep you on your toes. The only way to do that would be to keep surprising you whenever possible. And the best way to do that would be to break whatever patterns you guys had already picked up on."

Cam shook his head. By this time, Clint's eyesight was already good enough for him to see the big man's subtle movements. Things were still a bit blurry around the edges, but at least Clint could see edges again. That was a definite improvement from all the blindness he'd experienced this evening.

"Damn," Cam said softly. "He could've walked away from this place with a whole lot more of us lying dead on the ground. Usually, he only takes out one at a time, but he was sticking around. And he even got himself into position to fire on us again once we all thought he'd picked up and gone."

Fixing Clint with an earnest gaze, Cam said, "I owe you one helluva debt, Adams. If you weren't here, lord only knows how many more Jessup could've killed."

"Don't take this the wrong way," Clint said while

blinking away the last of the glowing red sparks. "But I'd save my thanks if I were you. Jessup's still out there. And now he knows that he'll have to hide better the next time he decides to go hunting." More to himself than to Cam, he added, "I only wish I could've done more."

"Oh, you've done more than you think." In response to Clint's questioning look, Cam squatted down and reached under the porch. When he pulled his hand back, he showed it to Clint.

Clint's eyesight might not have been completely back, but he could recognize blood when he saw it.

"He might have gotten away," Cam said. "But it looks like you got a piece of him before he did."

Despite all the things he'd done and all the many ways he'd earned his reputation, Clint liked to think that he wasn't a violent man. But even he couldn't deny that seeing that blood on Cam's fingers felt good. In fact, it felt even better when he remembered the way Jessup had squirmed when he'd been shot in the shoulder.

That part felt best of all.

THIRTY-SEVEN

"How much blood is down there?" Clint asked.

"A fair amount, but not enough to start celebrating just yet. I'd say he's hurt enough to put him down for at least the rest of the night."

"Then that's good enough for me." Blinking away some of the stinging at the edges of his eyes, Clint rubbed them with his palms and took a slow look around. "The flash burn is wearing off."

"You need any help getting back to your room?" Cam asked.

"Nah, I'll be fine."

"Not even a cane?"

Clint looked over to the other man and reared back his arm as though he was going to give Cam a taste of the back of his hand. "The last thing I need tonight is a smart-ass."

Holding up his hands, Cam grinned and took a few steps back. "Just testing to see if you're back in fighting shape. Looks like you passed. We're riding out tomorrow. Should we save you a spot in the group?"

"Do you think Jessup is going to follow you?"

146

"That's the idea. If we pull out of here, he'll come with us. At least for a while, anyway."

"Are you sure about that?"

Cam nodded. "Trust me. We've been dealing with this savage for a while."

"Then I'll be coming with you. But don't wait around for me. If I'm not there when you leave, I'll catch up."

"It'll be good to have you along, Adams. We're going to be heading north just after sunup. The trail runs through a stretch of woods and a couple shallow ravines."

"But that sounds like a perfect place for another ambush," Clint said.

"Like I said before . . . that's the idea. We don't have a lot of men left, in case you haven't noticed. Since we haven't had a lot of luck hunting him down, we've got to lure him out and force his hand. By the looks of what happened here tonight, it seems Jessup is getting anxious."

Cam let out a tired sigh. "And if we all stay here, someone's gonna get hurt that doesn't even have a place in this. I know I speak for the others when I say that I'd rather risk my own life than have someone innocent get killed. One way or another . . . this thing's gotta end."

Clint didn't like the sound of that plan. But he also recognized the look on Cam's face well enough to know that he was a determined man who was dead-set on the path he'd chosen. As foolhardy as it might have been for the group to bare their throats to a killer that was hungry for blood, he had to admire Cam for taking that risk in order to keep others safe.

Having been so close to that killer had shown Clint a lot. He knew that Cam was right. Jessup was desperate. He didn't need a clean look at the other man's face to see that. In fact, he could smell it. Also, he didn't need to look for his proof any more that Cam's story was accurate. Jessup himself had given him more than enough to satisfy Clint's curiosity.

And in doing that, the killer had made one big mistake. He'd pulled Clint so far into the hunt that there was only one way out.

"You're right," Clint said. "This ends tomorrow."

THIRTY-EIGHT

In some strange way, despite all that had happened over the last hour, Clint felt somehow better when he was walking back to the boardinghouse where he was staying. He'd been shot at, cut with a razor and nearly killed more times than he could rightly remember, but he still felt better than he had when he'd left his room earlier that night.

As much as he hated to admit it, he knew that he felt that way because he'd come to know the way Jessup worked a little better after having dealt with the killer. He'd looked into those eyes and had been close enough to smell the blood on his hands. Something like that didn't just happen to a man without changing him even a little bit. On the contrary, it had given Clint a little glimpse into how Jessup thought.

Like boxers who could recognize each other by the way they fought, Clint and Jessup had made a connection by locking horns. And because of that, Clint knew that Jessup had done his best for the night and would not be a bother until he'd had a chance to rest up and lick his wounds.

Clint wasn't sure exactly *how* he knew.

He just did.

There would be more confrontations between Jessup and the men hunting him . . . but not tonight. Knowing that was enough to let Clint head back to his room in good conscience and try to get some sleep before the killer got his hackles up once again.

Stepping up to the front door, Clint tried to pull it open and found it locked. "Aww, no," he groaned under his breath as all the comfort he'd built up inside himself quickly drifted away. Clint tried the door again just in case it might have jammed, but he could hear the latch smacking against the frame and knew that he really was locked away from that soft, comfortable bed inside his nice little room.

Out of sheer frustration, he leaned forward and smacked his head against the door. The next thing he knew, he was staggering forward as the door was pulled open. It took all of his reflexes to keep him from falling flat onto his face.

Standing just inside the boardinghouse, Eliza pulled the door the rest of the way open and jumped to one side as Clint came stumbling in. She put a hand over her mouth to conceal her laughter once she realized who it was and what Clint had just done.

"Are you all right?" she asked after she'd fought to contain her amusement.

Clint froze in place once he'd managed to stop his momentum. Another couple of steps and he would have knocked over some of Mrs. Tristip's shelves. As it was, he'd already made more noise than an elephant rampaging through a windowpane.

"Yeah," he said with as much dignity as he could manage under the circumstances. "I'm just fine. How are you?"

"Actually, I've been worried sick. We heard the shooting and Mrs. Tristip locked all the doors. I knew you hadn't come back yet and so I waited to let you in." Eliza dropped her gaze momentarily and then look back up at Clint. "I was hoping you weren't hurt."

Just then, she noticed the blood on Clint's shirt. "Oh, my god," she gasped. "You *are* hurt!"

"I'm fine. Really. It's just a—"

But Eliza was already rushing forward to see for herself. She opened his coat a little wider and felt the cut near the bottom of Clint's ribs. When she pulled back her hand and saw the blood on her own fingers, she didn't seem to be affected by it. Instead, she touched his wound gently until she'd felt it from one end to another.

"It's deep," she said as her eyes took in every part of him. "Is this the only one?"

Although Clint wanted to get some rest and tend to his wounds on his own, he couldn't deny the fact that he enjoyed Eliza's tender attention. Her hands felt good on his skin and her concern for him felt genuine enough to make him feel better just by being around her.

"Actually," Clint said in a voice that sounded a bit more painful than he actually felt, "I think he also got me on my leg."

Eliza looked down first to one leg and then the other. When she saw the trace of blood on the back of Clint's ankle, she bent down slightly to get a better look. "You're right. That does look like something cut through your boot. How far did you walk on that leg?"

"Only a couple blocks or so."

Stepping up so that she was standing with her side against Clint's, Eliza wrapped one arm around his shoulders and held it in place with her other hand. "You're coming upstairs with me."

"But I just—"

"I won't hear anything of it. I've worked in enough saloons for enough years to know how to tend to a few cuts like those. Are you shot?"

Clint shook his head. Even though he wasn't quite

milking the fact that he was hurt, he did allow his voice to falter ever so slightly when he said, "I don't think so, but I was just going to get some rest. I can see a doctor tomorrow morning."

"Don't be such a baby," Eliza replied. "Come upstairs with me and I can fix you up just as good. What's the matter? Don't you believe me?"

She was already starting to drag him toward the stairs. Of course, by this time, Clint wasn't really putting up much of a struggle. He didn't lean much of his weight upon her slender frame, but he allowed her to think that she was helping to keep his balance. Actually, that part wasn't hard to do after his unusual entrance.

"You really don't have to do this," Clint said.

Eliza looked up into his eyes and smiled. Right then, she showed that she wasn't really buying into the exaggerated performance he'd been giving her. Instead, she simply looked as though she enjoyed being near him just as much as he enjoyed being near her.

"I know," she replied. "But I want to. And if you'd rather just go back to your room and sleep . . . let me know."

Clint didn't say anything. He leaned a bit on Eliza and let her take him up the stairs to her own room. When they were about to go inside, he asked, "What about . . ."

"Sadie? She should be fine. Don't worry about her. I'd rather have you all to myself."

THIRTY-NINE

The first thing Clint noticed was that Eliza's room was easily twice as big as his own. The bed looked like it could sleep three comfortably and there was more furniture in there than some people had in their houses. Both dressers looked like they might have been antiques. A brass wash basin sat on top of an ornately carved end table. There was even a writing desk complete with a stack of paper and envelopes.

"I've lived here for over a year," Eliza said when she noticed the expression on Clint's face. "I guess Mrs. Tristip figures that gives me seniority." She led him to the edge of her bed and sat him down. Running her fingers through his hair, she added, "But don't be too upset. You can stay here for no extra charge."

Clint felt like he wanted to kiss her, but before he could act on it, Eliza pulled away and went to the table and filled the wash basic from a large white pitcher. She moved about the room, gathering up some cloths as well as a needle and thread before bringing everything to Clint's side.

"Here, let me," she said as she reached out and took Clint's coat off his shoulders. Eliza let her hands brush

153

along his neck and arms as she helped remove the coat, allowing them to linger just a bit longer than necessary.

Clint didn't mind in the least. In fact, he sat back and let her do all the work. The pain in his side had died down to a dull throb, shot through occasionally with a sharper jolt. That pain was easily forgotten when he saw that she'd already started unbuttoning his shirt.

The expression on Eliza's face was warm and seductive. She was careful not to hurt him, but her eyes seemed more attracted to the skin that she was uncovering rather than the bloody cut farther down his torso. Once his shirt was gone, she soaked a rag in some water and pressed it gently to his side.

"Is that better?" she asked.

Nodding, Clint said, "Yes it is. You really do seem to know what you're doing."

Eliza put on a mildly offended expression. "Did you think I just did this to get you into my room?"

"No. Of course not." Clint paused a second or two before adding, "If you wanted to do that, all you had to do was ask."

A little smile drifted onto Eliza's face, but she kept her head down while gently dabbing away the blood from Clint's wound. After wringing out the cloth, she rubbed it along Clint's torso, over his stomach, and then up onto his chest. "That's not too bad." Pulling her eyes back down to the cut, she said, "Your wound, I mean. It looks kind of deep, but not too bad at all. I can stitch it up for you . . . if you trust me to do the job right."

Clint did have a few reservations, but he didn't feel like voicing them at the moment. The fact of the matter was that he actually didn't feel like getting up and leaving her room. "Go ahead," he told her. "But if I start to scream, you'd better stop."

Eliza smiled again before picking up the needle and thread. "All right then. Here I go."

Her hands were slow, strong and steadier than some doctors Clint had been to in the past. Although it didn't feel great to have her work the needle through the edges of his skin, she took so much care with her task that Clint enjoyed watching her work.

She was done before he knew it. Eliza bit off the end of the thread, tied a small knot and placed her hand over the wound. "How's that?" she asked. "I hope it feels better than before at least."

"It sure does." Clint took a moment to really inspect the stitches. "I'll be damned. You really did a great job. How can I repay you?"

"You don't have to repay me."

"Well, I can't just leave here without giving you something."

Eliza's eyes were like deep brown pools. They roamed over Clint's bare skin before moving back up to lock on to Clint's. That sly, sexy smile was back, letting him know that she know exactly where he was headed. The way she leaned in closer to him told Clint that she didn't mind going there with him one bit.

"I don't want you to give me anything," she said, cutting him off at the pass. "But if you want, you can take this."

And just as Clint was about to get disappointed, he saw Eliza lean in and plant a kiss on his lips that nearly took his breath away. Her soft, full lips seemed to melt onto his. The longer they kissed, the more intense it felt and soon there was a heat being generated between them that could have melted away every bit of snow that was lying on the ground outside their window.

Eliza let her hands wander over Clint's chest, her fingers drifting on his skin before slipping around his waist. Accidentally, she grazed the stitches she'd just sewn, causing Clint to jump back onto the bed.

"Oh, I'm so sorry," she said.

"It's all right," Clint replied, fighting back the wince that had twisted his face. "Just . . . give me a minute here."

When she saw that the wound wasn't bleeding, Eliza knew that she hadn't done any fresh damage. She stepped back and pressed her shoulders against the door, making sure that it was shut tight and locked. "All right. I'll give you some time. But while you're waiting, I can at least give you something to look at."

Clint moved back on the bed and kicked off his boots. The shallow cut on the back of his ankle was all but forgotten the instant he saw what Eliza was doing.

First, she shrugged out of the shawl that had been wrapped around her shoulders and let it fall to the floor. Then she placed her hands on her hips and moved them slowly up along her sides, stopping once she could trace her fingertips along the upper edge of her dress. She arched her back and tilted her head upward while turning in a half circle so that she was facing the wall. From there, she began to slowly unfasten her dress.

Finally, after the dress came loose, she wriggled in just the right way so that the garment fell to the floor around her feet. Turning to look at Clint over her shoulder, Eliza's face was framed by the soft hair which flowed down along her back. "Feeling better now?" she asked. "Or would you rather I left you to your sleep?"

"If you don't get over here, I might have to bust these stitches to come and get you."

FORTY

Eliza's body was trim and slender, her muscles moving gracefully beneath her skin as she stepped out of her discarded dress and walked over to the bedside. Every step caused her hips to twitch enticingly and her full, rounded breasts to bob slightly. The closer she got to him, the harder her little nipples became, giving away just how excited she was to get into Clint's arms.

The only things she was still wearing were her knee-high boots and a pair of silk lace panties. Already, the filmy material was clinging to her skin.

"I'm here," she whispered. "What do you want me to do now?"

"Finish undressing for me."

Lifting one foot and setting it onto the mattress within Clint's reach, Eliza said, "Go ahead and do it then."

"No. I want you to do it for me."

Letting her eyes linger on him for a second or two, Eliza turned her attention toward her own body and reached to unbutton her boot. The little buttons ran down the outside of her leg and when she got halfway down on the first one, she was stopped by Clint's voice.

"No," he said. "Leave those on." When Eliza looked

157

up at him with an intrigued expression, Clint said, "You
look awful good in those. I'd hate to see you take them
off."

She shrugged casually. "Suit yourself."

Eliza set her foot back down onto the floor and took a
step back away from the bed. Hooking her thumbs
through the sides of her panties, she started peeling them
down over her hips. Just as she exposed the top edge of
dark hair between her legs, she pivoted slowly on the balls
of her feet until her back was facing Clint.

Glancing over her shoulder, Eliza seemed very satisfied
with the frustration she saw in Clint's face. After looking
away from him, she shook her hair over her shoulders so
that it cascaded down her naked back. Then, bending at
the knees, she slid the panties down her thighs and over
her half-buttoned boots.

Despite the fact that Clint wanted to touch her so bad
that he could damn near taste it, he was enjoying the show
immensely. Her body was exquisitely trim and wriggled
invitingly as she stepped out of her panties and rose back
up to a standing position.

From there, Eliza turned slowly around. Her firm buttocks shifted in a sensuous rhythm and before she exposed
her front to him, she covered her breasts with one arm
and tossed the panties to him with the other.

Clint looked away for only a second so he could catch
the frilly lace underwear. It felt just as soft as her skin
looked and carried her sweet, vaguely musky scent. When
he looked up again, she had already placed her other hand
across her waist. She held her head low in a demure pose.
Even though Clint knew she was anything but demure,
the look on her face was undeniably sexy.

"Good lord," Clint said as he let his eyes wander up
and down Eliza's body. "You look beautiful."

"Keeping the boots on makes me feel naughty," she
said in a low voice. "Kind of like I'm being a bad girl."

"You haven't done anything bad as far as I can see."

"Oh really?" Eliza pulled her hands away, allowing her fingertips to graze lightly over her breasts and vagina. "We'll have to see if we can do something to change that."

FORTY-ONE

Eliza lunged forward, dropping herself down on top of Clint and forcing both of them down onto the bed. Their lips met in a passionate kiss that seemed to go on for hours. Her mouth was hot and sweet at the same time and she couldn't seem to get enough of him as they tasted each other amid her soft, satisfied moans.

As soon as she broke away from him, she was busy pulling off the rest of Clint's clothes and tossing them in random directions around the room. The instant she was done with that, she started kissing the inside of Clint's thighs, quickly working her way up to his rigid penis. Eliza looked at him for a second and moved her hands around the base of his cock. Then, while looking up into his eyes, she parted her lips and took him into her mouth.

She lowered her head all the way down until she had swallowed his entire shaft. From there, she tightened her lips around him and slowly moved up while her tongue massaged his most sensitive areas along the way. Stopping to suck on just the tip of him, she let out a contented groan which heightened his pleasure even more.

Unable to contain himself for another moment, Clint reached down and guided her closer to him. Once he got his hands on her hips, he pulled her around so that she could straddle his face while still looking toward his feet. All Clint had to do was pull her down and lift his head up slightly and he could taste her.

The instant she felt his tongue moving between her legs, Eliza closed her eyes and arched her back, savoring the way Clint tasted her while she pumped her hips back and forth. When she opened her eyes again, she lowered her mouth over Clint's rod and bobbed her head up and down, sucking him loudly.

When Eliza straightened up again, she started to say something, but her breath was taken away by a wave of pleasure which pulsed through her body as Clint's tongue flicked over her clit. That wave went right into another and before she knew what was happening, she was grinding her pussy against Clint's tongue in the throes of a powerful orgasm.

Clint felt as though he could play Eliza's body like a finely tuned instrument. And once he felt that her climax had subsided a bit, he moved out from underneath her and flipped her over onto her back. She landed roughly upon the mattress, but her eyes flashed with excitement as Clint loomed over her.

"We should be quiet," she whispered. "These walls aren't very thick."

"You can try to be quiet," Clint said as he spread open her legs and got between them. "But I'll do my best to make you scream." And with that, he thrust his penis into her waiting vagina. The lips between her legs were so moist that he slid easily inside of her and he didn't stop until he couldn't drive forward another inch.

Eliza's eyes were open wide and she reached up over her head to grip the headboard with both hands. When Clint slammed into her, the pleasure was so intense that she almost did cry out. The only thing that kept her from doing just that was biting down on her lower lips and thrusting her head back into the pillows.

Taking hold of her hips with both hands, Clint straightened up so that he was kneeling on the mattress and lifting her up so he could pump into her again and again. He stopped for a minute so he could get a good look at her and run his hands all over her body.

Clint took his time feeling the smooth texture of her bare skin. Her stomach was flat and taut as it rose and fell with every excited breath. Her breasts were firm and heaving as well, capped with firm, erect nipples. But what Clint liked the most was her legs. After running his hands back down along her sides, he came to the tops of her boots which was the only thing she still wore.

Since she'd left them on at his request, the boots felt especially good beneath Clint's hands. The rough leather was a stark contrast to Eliza's silky skin and she seemed as though she was aching to pull them off so she could be completely naked as he made love to her. But the torture was exquisite and for that reason alone, Clint kept them on. In fact, he enjoyed the way those boots felt when she wrapped her legs around his waist.

He started pumping again. Slowly at first, but quickly building to a fast rhythm which they both used to their mutual advantage. She thrust her hips forward as he slid inside of her, pulling back at the same time so they could repeat the motions faster and faster.

Clint leaned down so he could gently kiss her nipples. When he let his teeth graze over the sensitive skin, he heard Eliza pull in a sharp breath and grab hold of the back of his head. Taking that as a signal, Clint licked the fleshy nubs before gently biting them, his hips still thrusting between her thighs.

Every part of Eliza's body struggled to keep her from screaming in ecstasy. Her legs tensed and held on to him tightly. Her stomach became tight with shallow breaths and strained to keep up the rhythm of their lovemaking. She began to dig her nails into Clint's back and she wriggled against the mattress as another orgasm started to work its way beneath her flesh.

She knew that when she climaxed again, she would not be able to keep herself quiet. And more as a little game between herself and Clint, she pulled her face in close to Clint's shoulders and pressed her mouth against his skin so she could maintain her relative silence.

As her second orgasm swept through her, Eliza's muscles tightened all at once. Clint could feel her tightening around his cock as he pumped it into her one last time. He could also feel her teeth scraping against his skin as she pressed herself tightly against him and let out a muffled groan of sheer pleasure.

Reacting to her, Clint's body started to pulse with excitement as well. The sensation of Eliza grinding against him as he was wrapped in her arms and legs and enveloped within the wet lips between her thighs was suddenly almost too much for him to bear. His own pleasure built to a climax and he exploded inside of her.

The feeling was so intense that Clint almost let out a moan that filled the entire room. But he was playing the game as well and when he felt the exclamation coming up from the back of his throat, he buried his face in her hair and groaned until he was fully satiated.

Once both of them were spent, they fell apart from each other as if the force holding them together had suddenly been turned off. Clint and Eliza landed side by side on the mattress, neither one of them willing or able to even move so they were under the covers.

"Good lord." Eliza sighed.

All Clint was able to say was, "Yeah. Me too."

Looking over at him, she smiled widely and sat up. "I think Mrs. Tristip might've heard us."

Shrugging, Clint said, "And I think I couldn't care less."

Eliza pulled her knees up close to her chest and wrapped her arms around them. "Can I take these boots off now?"

"I guess so. But don't throw them too far . . . we might need them in a bit."

Eliza pouted a little bit but once she'd removed the boots, she was careful to set them right next to the bed where they were easily within arm's reach.

FORTY-TWO

Sadie had tried going to sleep once she'd gotten back to her room. She'd tried, but all she got for her troubles was a cramp in her back after lying down for too long after her eyes refused to shut. Despite all her efforts, she simply couldn't get the image of that strange man out of her mind.

Normally, whenever she didn't like one of her customers, it was a simple matter of pushing their faces out of her mind until it was shortly forgotten. But there was something else about that man. It was something vaguely familiar.

Yes. She realized just then that he *was* familiar. She hadn't thought so at first, but now she knew that she'd seen him somewhere before. Perhaps around town or in passing, but not somewhere she normally went. It was one of those things that bothered her more and more as she kept thinking about it. And since she knew she wasn't about to forget it while staring up at her ceiling, she pulled on her shawl and coat and headed outside for a walk.

The fresh air felt good at first, but soon the cold had sunk its teeth all the way down to her bones and her shoulders began to shake. Suddenly, just as she was about

to turn around and head back inside, she spotted someone
standing across the street near the boardinghouse where
Eliza stayed.

He wasn't particularly threatening, but she did find it
odd the way he stood in the middle of the freezing winds
with his arms crossed like a lifeless statue. The figure
hardly moved, even when the wind picked up a few stray
pieces of snow and blew them against the exposed skin
of his face.

Sadie was about to turn away from him when she noticed something that made her pause. It wasn't much more
than a glimpse of black beneath the man's knee-length
jacket as well as a hint of white around his neck. Already,
she could feel her troubles lightening on her shoulders as
she walked up and approached the figure she'd spotted.

"Excuse me," she said timidly.

The man didn't seem to notice her. Instead, he was
staring up intently at one of the windows on the second
floor of the boardinghouse.

Sadie walked up closer, this time reaching out to place
a hand on his shoulder before speaking again. "Pardon
me. Can I talk to you, Father?"

Twitching as though he was startled by the touch of
Sadie's hand, Father Planter spun around to glare at her.
For a fleeting moment, the look in his eyes was full of
anger. His voice was tainted with dark emotion as well at
first, but quickly softened as he snapped, "What is it?"

Sadie recoiled instinctively. "I'm sorry. I didn't mean
to . . ." Her mouth froze and her blood ran colder than
anything the winter could produce. She stood there with
her hand still outstretched. Every bit of color seeped out
of her skin and recognition reflected in her eyes. "Oh . . .
my God."

"I'm sorry you had to see me like this, child," Father
Planter said. "But now I'm afraid I can't allow you to
leave until we've had a little talk."

• • •

A single gunshot sounded in the nearly empty street. Unlike the explosions that had rolled through the town earlier in the evening, this one was muffled and alone. There was no sound of a struggle before it came and no rushing footsteps after it had faded away.

Just a solitary *thump* and the crunch of a body falling onto the packed snow.

In an hour or so, the front door to the boardinghouse came open and Mrs. Tristip poked her face outside. She was known to step onto her front porch to enjoy an occasional cigarette when nobody could see her, but this time she didn't even get a chance to strike a match before spotting the crumpled form lying on the side of the street.

The old woman's shrill scream filled the night as soon as she saw who was lying in the snow. She tried waving her hand in front of Sadie's face and even shaking the young woman, but to no avail. The girl was dead. Once Mrs. Tristip knew that for certain, she began screaming all over again and this time she couldn't stop until she felt a pair of strong hands physically turning her away from the corpse.

"What happened?" came a rough, male voice. "Mrs. Tristip! What happened here? Did you see who did this?"

There were more people around her now. After taking a deep breath, Mrs. Tristip struggled to look behind her and saw a familiar person bending down to look at the body.

"I . . . is that you, dearie?" the old woman asked.

Eliza looked up from Sadie's body, her expression looking every bit as disheveled as the clothes she'd hastily pulled on to cover herself. "It's me. Wh . . . what happened?" she asked in a weak, almost faraway voice.

Turning to look at whoever was holding her, Mrs. Tristip found herself staring up into the face of her newest boarder. She didn't know the man all that well, but she knew that she somehow felt safe around him. And when she saw the concern in his eyes, the old woman broke down into tears.

FORTY-THREE

Trying to comfort the old woman, Clint patted her on the back and motioned for Eliza to come over and take his place. Once she was close enough, he handed Mrs. Tristip to Eliza and stepped over to get a look at the body.

There was a gaping hole in Sadie's stomach. Already, the bloody maw was starting to turn black as the blood started to freeze. The snow where she'd fallen was dark red with a pool of collected blood.

Clint took a closer look at the body and noticed right away that there was a black scorch mark around the wound, letting him know that whoever had shot her had done so at point-blank range. There wasn't a lot he could gather from the scene. Being on a well-traveled street, there were too many footprints to pick out the killer's tracks and recent snowfall made it hard to even find any tracks that were fresher than others.

Giving the old woman a chance to collect herself, Clint turned to her one more time and asked, "Did you see what happened, Mrs. Tristip? Did you see anything at all?"

"I was looking out the window a while ago and I saw Father Planter standing outside. Sadie was across the street, but then I went back to my room and when I came out again . . . I found her . . . like . . . like this."

Clint took in the old woman's words and didn't think there was anything that she'd said that could help him. But then he hit upon something in particular that made him straighten up and take notice. "Wait a second. You said that you saw Father Planter out here?"

Mrs. Tristip nodded her head. "Yes I did. He's walked by here a lot ever since he came to town."

"And you saw him how long ago?"

"I don't know. Maybe an hour."

Clint knew it had been several hours since he'd met up with the priest on his way to the boardinghouse. And even then, Planter had told him he was leaving to go home for the night.

"And how long ago did he get to town?"

Mrs. Tristip seemed confused by Clint's question, but she still did her best to answer it. After mulling it over for a few seconds, she replied, "No more than a month ago, that's for certain. He just helps Father Samms around the chapel. Sometimes he takes confessions, but mostly he just lends a hand when he's needed. From what I hear, he travels around a lot. Why do you want to know about him?"

Suddenly, the pieces he'd been given were starting to fall into place. He now was certain he'd solved at least one mystery that had been bothering him. Mrs. Tristip was talking to him and asking him questions, but Clint's mind was racing too quickly for him to think about answering her properly.

A sense of dire urgency flooded through Clint's body and he spun around so he could hurry back into the boardinghouse. Once inside, he all but flew up the stairs and rushed into Eliza's room so he could fetch the rest of his clothes. By the time he was fully dressed, Eliza was standing breathless in the doorway.

"What's the matter with you?" she asked. "You look like you just saw a ghost."

"I know who killed Sadie," he said as he buckled on his gun belt. "And if he's who I think he is, he might very well be leaving town right now. Hell, he might already be gone."

"Who is it?"

"I don't have the time right now."

"Why would he kill Sadie?"

Clint stopped and looked straight into Eliza's eyes. "I'm not sure why, but if he did, that means he's desperate. And if he's desperate, then that means he might have considered her a threat. Maybe she saw something . . ."

Eliza snapped her fingers. "She said she was with a man tonight who frightened her. She was more scared than I ever saw her."

"Why was she frightened?"

"She said he was just . . . scary. Like he was mean or something. I don't know, but in our business, a girl needs to trust her instincts or she'll get hurt real bad, real quick."

"Yeah," Clint said as he checked the Colt's cylinder. "I find that's true in my line of work as well." Holstering the gun, he took both of Eliza's hands in his and spoke in a steady tone. "This part is real important. Did Sadie attend church services? Or maybe even go to confession?"

Eliza looked as confused by Clint's question as Mrs. Tristip had, but she also did her best to oblige him. "No. She never went to church. Sadie always said she had no business going to church after spending all her days and nights in a saloon. I think she felt ashamed about herself and being with a priest would only make her feel worse." A chill seemed to run through Eliza's body and she rubbed her arms as if to keep herself warm. "Why would you ask such a thing?"

"I can't explain right now, but thank you," Clint said just before leaning in to kiss her quickly on the lips. "Thanks for all you've done to help me."

And without another word, Clint was gone.

FORTY-FOUR

The first thing Clint did was take a quick search of the area around the boardinghouse. For some reason, Father Planter seemed to be attracted to this area. It could have been any number of things, but Clint didn't have the time to find out why. All he needed to know was that there was nobody lurking around in the shadows at the moment. Once he was certain of that, he made his way toward the town's chapel.

Clint made sure to keep off the main streets. Instead, he moved as though he was on the run, sticking to alleys and darkened walkways. He wasn't familiar with Allyn's Mill enough to know every route through town, but he figured he'd have better luck in finding the man he was after that way than by simply charging down the street for anyone to see.

Although he didn't find any killers in the shadows, Clint did make it to the chapel in less time than he'd thought possible. He'd seen the small building on his way into town. It was built in the same fashion as many places of worship. It almost resembled a small, square-shaped house with clean white walls and a single stained-glass window. A steeple loomed over the front entrance, topped with a simple wooden cross. Clint walked straight through the front door and headed for the first person he could see.

Before he got there, Clint saw the room's single occupant spin around to look at him with a surprised look on his face. "Can I help you, my son?"

Clint studied the other man's face and said, "Where's Father Planter?"

The priest looked to be in his late sixties. His skin clung tightly to his face, which made him look like more of a scarecrow than a man. "I don't know. I provide a room for him when he's in town, but he hasn't been around much over the last few days."

"Did you see him at all today?"

"Why yes," the priest said. "In fact, he told me he might be leaving for a while. He travels a lot to spread the word of God to towns much smaller than these. Strange thing, though. When I did see him earlier this evening, it looked as though he might have been injured. I offered to bring the doctor here, but he refused. He was quite adamant about it. I've been concerned about him and it's very nice to see that someone else feels the same way."

Clint had been about to leave the church, but paused to ask another question. "Tell me, Father . . . when he travels, would other people give him food and a place to stay?"

"Almost certainly. Missionaries often have to rely on the kindness of others."

"Thank you, Father. You've given me another piece to work with."

The priest didn't know what Clint was talking about, but he was glad he could be of service. After all, the younger man did seem to be in better spirits when he left than when he'd first come through the church's doors. Rather than try to figure out why Clint might have been in such a hurry, the priest returned to what he'd been doing.

If the young man was troubled, he would surely be seeing him again at his next mass.

Clint broke into a run after he left the church. Rather than try to search any more within a town he didn't know, he made a straight line for the stables. As soon as he got there, he saddled Eclipse himself and tossed some money at the livery keeper as he rode back out into the night.

He didn't think the man he was after was hiding in town anymore. If his hunch was correct, his target had left a while ago in a rush. Clint knew he had to be sure, which was why he'd gone to the church. But after discovering that Father Planter wasn't there, his only hope was to catch him on horseback.

Even if Planter did have a good head start, Clint put enough faith in Eclipse to know that he still had a chance in catching up with him. The only question now was where Planter might have ridden in the time he'd been given.

The answer to that seemed well out of Clint's reach at first, but it only took a bit of creative thinking to narrow down some of his choices. Clint was in a hurry, so rather than take his time to ponder, he spoke through all the possibilities out loud.

"Sadie was killed up-close and in a hurry. Once that was done, her killer would be in a hurry too, which means he would want to get out of town and as far away as possible as quickly as he could manage."

Shutting his eyes tightly, Clint pictured Allyn's Mill as though he was looking at a large map filled in with all the details he knew about the area.

"He probably doesn't think anyone's on to him, so he would just want to move quickly rather than quietly. That means he would be riding on a trail instead of through any rough terrain. It's the middle of a damn cold night, so that definitely means he'll be on a trail.

"He'll want to go to a town rather than camp . . . and the closest town is . . ." Clint's eyes snapped open and a sly grin appeared on his face. "The closest town is three miles north."

When he said it, Clint felt from his gut instincts that he'd hit upon the right answer. In fact, he could almost picture the other man riding on the narrow trail in the cold, pitch blackness.

Since he didn't have the time to second-guess himself, Clint touched his heels to Eclipse's sides and sent the Darley Arabian charging out of town. He took the trail that led north from Allyn's Mill, hoping that he hadn't already let his target get too far out of his reach.

He hadn't even been riding for a minute or two before he spotted a figure on a horse about twenty yards ahead. Clint focused his eyes on the solitary rider and drew back on the reins as he got a little closer. His hand was already hanging close to the modified Colt at his side and he was ready for anything.

Sensing this, the figure stopped . . . turned around . . . and revealed himself.

FORTY-FIVE

Clint was just about to draw when he spotted a familiar face beneath the hat setting forward upon the figure's head. Letting out a deep breath, he brought Eclipse to a stop and pulled up alongside the other man.

"Glad you have a good eye, Adams," Gordon said. "I think it just saved my life."

"You thought right," Clint replied. "Now what are you doing out here?"

"I heard about the woman that got killed, so I rousted my men one more time so we could possibly finish that animal off."

"What made you think that girl had anything to do with Jessup?"

"It's too much of a coincidence to have her get killed on the same night that that animal bares his fangs. And I'm not much of one for coincidences."

"Me either," Clint agreed.

"What about you? What brings you out this way? And don't tell me it's a coincidence."

Before Clint could answer, another rider came galloping toward Gordon from farther up the trail. He was out

of breath when he came to a stop and Clint recognized
him as Sanchez.

"Rico and I spotted someone riding farther up this trail.
He's alone."

"How far is he?" Clint asked.

Sanchez took a moment to look at Clint and when he
recognized him, he replied, "Not far. He's in a hurry, but
he wasn't riding his horse too hard."

"I'll bet he wasn't," Clint said. "He's not planning on
stopping until he reaches the next town."

Gordon's eyes narrowed. "Was it Jessup?"

"Couldn't say," Sanchez answered. "You said to let you
know when we found anyone. Rico and Connoway are
up the road a piece and will take him down if I give a
signal."

Gordon was starting to say something, but Clint
stopped him with a hand on his shoulder. "If you don't
mind, I've got a way we might be able to handle this."

At first, Gordon seemed hesitant. But then he nodded
and said, "Cam spoke highly of you . . . and that's the
only reason I'm doing this. Let's hear your plan, but make
it quick."

Father Planter snapped the reins against his horse's neck,
even though he knew the animal was plenty tired already.
The cold bit into both of them even worse than usual since
the air didn't even retain the memory of sunlight. It was
a few hours until dawn, which meant that the cold didn't
get much worse than it was at that moment. For that reason, he'd been trying to keep his horse moving, but not
at full speed. The last thing he needed right now was to
have the animal collapse.

At that moment, there was a rumbling sound which
seemed to come from all around him. It resembled faraway thunder, but it wasn't coming from the clouds over-

head. In fact, when he looked up, he saw there were no clouds overhead.

Before he had a chance to listen too carefully, the priest heard some more of that rumbling coming up on him from behind. He turned in his saddle and squinted at the darkness until his eyes picked out the shape of a man approaching him on horseback.

Whoever it was, they were riding their animal to its limit. Even from this distance, Planter could see the steam pumping from the horse's mouth and nostrils like it was being expelled from a train's engine. Since he knew his horse was getting tired anyway, Planter let the animal rest while the other man got a chance to catch up. Perhaps if he could see what this man wanted, he might be able to ask for some help into town.

The rider slowed down once he got close and came to a stop. Planter recognized him immediately.

"Hello there, Mister Adams. What brings you out here on such a cold evening?"

"Why'd you kill the girl?" Clint asked.

Planter's face dropped. "What? I . . . I don't know—"

"Skip the bullshit," Clint interrupted. "Why are you riding in the middle of the night? Trying to get somewhere else that will shelter you for a few days? I'll bet that's why you became a priest in the first place. But that would be giving you too much credit, wouldn't it? I'm sure you just took those clothes off a dead body after you put a bullet through the real priest's head."

Father Planter still looked shocked, but another kind of tension was coming over his face.

Clint saw this and went on. "I don't know why you were lurking outside my boardinghouse, but I have a real good idea of why you did the rest of what you did." He moved Eclipse up a little closer until he was only a foot or two away from the other man. "That girl didn't attend church on a regular basis which is why she didn't know exactly who you were, but Eliza knew . . ."

Suddenly Clint's eyes lit up as a revelation sank home inside his mind. "*That's* why you were outside that boarding house. She knew who you were . . . that's why she wouldn't sleep with you. But Sadie didn't recognize you without your black-and-white clothes on, so she took you and showed you a great time. But I heard that you scared her. She didn't know why, but you scared her." Clint leaned in and slapped his hand on the priest's left shoulder and held on even as the other man squirmed in intense pain.

"She was scared because she could feel the killer in you," Clint said. "And when you ran into her outside the boardinghouse, she recognized you and saw the outfit you were wearing. And you killed her because you couldn't take the chance of her telling any more to anyone else . . . especially to those men hunting you. Right, Jessup?"

The priest shook his head even as the blood was soaking through his jacket.

"A priest can drift from town to town with ease, can't he?" Clint said. "He even gets room and board from good people trying to do right by their church. That was how you could disappear so well all this time when Gordon and Cam were hunting you down. That was how you could blend in so well right under their noses. Folks like Cam and the rest of those men are looking for a killer, not a priest. And that, combined with your skills at hiding in ambush like a coward were all you needed."

The priest started to squirm and reach around on the side of his saddle. "No! I could never harm another soul!"

"I said save the bullshit! It all fits in too well." Clint locked his eyes on to the priest's. "I stared into your eyes tonight when you were trying to kill me. I shot you right *here*," he said, squeezing the wound beneath the priest's jacket. "And I'll bet my last bit of proof is right *here*." With that, Clint reached out and took hold of both of the priest's wrists. It was a bit of a struggle, but Clint's speed was more than a match for the struggling man.

When Clint got a grip on the other man's wrists, he searched his sleeves for a second or two before he'd found what he wanted. With a quick snapping motion, Clint cracked the other man's arm like a whip, causing something thin and metallic to fall to the ground between both horses.

Triumphantly, Clint looked down and saw the folded straight razor lying revealed in the snow.

"Eureka," Clint whispered.

Jessup let the priest's face melt away, replacing it with a savage snarl. His foot came up in a desperate kick which dropped both men from their saddles. He flipped up a blanket to reveal the rifle beneath his saddlebag and levered a round into the chamber.

"Finding me is one thing," Jessup growled. "Taking me is another."

FORTY-SIX

Clint nearly took the toe of Jessup's boot directly in the spot where his freshly-stitched wound lay beneath his shirt. That attack was just another bit of proof in his mind that he'd gotten the right man. Rolling with the blow, Clint twisted his body to absorb the kick in a different spot as he also got himself in position to land on his feet once he fell off of Eclipse's back.

He hit the ground on both feet, crouching low while moving around Eclipse's flank. Not wanting to risk having Jessup put a bullet into the Darley Arabian, Clint slapped the stallion on the rump, which sent Eclipse away in a brisk gallop. When the horse had moved, he was just able to catch a glimpse of Jessup's rifle barrel poking from over his own horse's saddle.

Clint waited until the last possible moment before diving to one side. At that same instant, a shot cracked through the air, but not from the gun in Jessup's hands.

Instead, the shot came from the scattered groups of trees behind Clint and over his shoulder. The bullet hissed through the air like an angry hornet and clipped a piece off of Jessup's scalp directly over his right ear.

The killer was visibly stunned as he was forced to stagger back. A look of ferocious anger darkening his face, he brought the rifle back up to his shoulder and sighted down its barrel to take his shot.

A second shot popped from the distance, but this time it came from somewhere off to Jessup's right. This round dug a hole in the killer's thigh which exploded with a fine spray of blood and sent a sharp pain lancing through Jessup's entire side.

"What is this?" Jessup snarled.

Clint stood his ground, ready to act at a moment's notice. "It's called payback," he said. "And I'll let it go to the men who deserve it the most."

Jessup looked more like a cornered animal than a man. His eyes glazed over with the realization of what was going on blazing like a signal fire behind them. Gritting his teeth, he reeled around to get a look at any of the ones who'd shot him, but saw only Clint framed against the darkness.

"Doesn't feel too good, does it?" Clint asked. "It's sure a hell of a lot better being the one hiding than the one at this end of the sights, isn't it?"

"You . . ."

Shrugging, Clint said, "I'm not the one that's been hunting you down over all these years. But I am the one who played the part of wild card in the game. I just shook things up enough to tip the balance, that's all. The real credit goes to the ones who gave their lives to track you down.

"They were right, weren't they? Gordon and Cam said that you would just find someone else to kill if you weren't stopped. The dead girl back in town proved that. I wonder if you can answer one last question for me." Pausing, Clint looked around at the darkness which surrounded them like a frozen shroud. "Can you tell me who's next to die now?"

Jessup looked as though he was about to go off like a

stick of dynamite. His entire body trembled and he launched himself back with both legs. The motion sent his entire body flying backward as shots rang out from the shadows all around him.

Some of the bullets dug into his body, while others whipped through the air around him. But nothing would stop him before he did what he'd set his mind to do. No matter how much blood streamed from his fresh wounds, Jessup still brought that rifle up and grinned at Clint with crimson-stained teeth.

"Fuck you," Jessup spat and squeezed his trigger.

Clint's hand disappeared in a flicker of motion. In the fraction of a second after Jessup's finger tightened, Clint's Colt had cleared leather. The modified pistol barked once, sending a single round into Jessup's skull and dropping the killer flat on his back.

For the next couple of moments, Clint was surrounded by a calm breeze and the echo of gunfire fading away in all directions. Before too long, there came the snap of branches and the sound of snow being crunched under several boots.

One by one, Cam, Gordon and the rest of their men emerged from the positions they'd taken around Clint. They each carried a rifle in their hand as they walked up and formed a circle around the fallen killer. They looked down upon Jessup with expressions of relief mixed in with a healthy portion of fatigue.

"You think we got him?" Cam asked sarcastically.

Like most of the others, Clint couldn't take his eyes away from the body. "Only about a dozen times."

"Jesus, Adams," Gordon said as he stomped up to Clint's side. "You barely gave us any time to surround this place."

"I knew you'd make it."

"Yeah, well . . . thanks for waiting for us," Gordon said. "We needed to do this ourselves."

Clint looked up at the other man. "And you did. I didn't want any part of this fight of yours until I knew you men weren't feeding me a line."

"What changed your mind about that?"

"Watching you. Seeing that you really were doing everything you could to do what was right without getting anyone else hurt. The law could've helped you on this, but . . . I understand why you wanted to do this alone."

"Glad to hear that, Adams."

"Speaking of the law," Cam mentioned as he stepped forward. "I know you work with them quite a bit yourself."

"Yeah," Clint said. "What of it?"

"How much are they going to hear about this? My men and I still have prices on our heads for some of the jobs we pulled. I guess I'd like to know if you mean to collect."

Clint ignored the intense looks he was getting from all the other men. He knew they were there, and addressed them all when he spoke. "No. If I believe what you told me about Jessup, I might as well believe that you've all decided to change your ways."

Every one of the men nodded their approval. They all seemed to look at Clint as if he was one of their own; a brother tied to them by mutually spilled blood.

"Just remember one thing, though," Clint added in a steely voice. "If you men decide to take up your old ways and I hear about it . . . you *will* be hunted again. And that's a promise you'd all better believe."

Not another word was spoken between Clint and the surviving members of Gordon's crew. They nodded at Clint to show they understood what he'd told them. And they all stepped aside as he walked through them on his way to where Eclipse was waiting.

Watch for

THE MAKING OF A BAD MAN

252nd novel in the exciting GUNSMITH series
from Jove

Coming in December!

J. R. ROBERTS
THE
GUNSMITH